If the Witness Lied

OTHER BOOKS BY CAROLINE B. COONEY

Diamonds in the Shadow
A Friend at Midnight
Hit the Road
Code Orange
The Girl Who Invented Romance
Family Reunion
Goddess of Yesterday
For All Time
The Ransom of Mercy Carter
What Janie Found
Tune In Anytime
Burning Up
What Child Is This?
The Face on the Milk Carton
Whatever Happened to Janie?
The Voice on the Radio
Both Sides of Time
Out of Time
Prisoner of Time
Driver's Ed
Twenty Pageants Later
Among Friends

If the Witness Lied

CAROLINE B.
COONEY

DELACORTE PRESS

Copyright © 2009 by Caroline B. Cooney

All rights reserved. Published in the United States by Delacorte Press, an imprint of Random House Children's Books, a division of Random House, Inc., New York.

Delacorte Press is a registered trademark and the colophon is a trademark of Random House, Inc.

Visit us on the Web! www.randomhouse.com/teens
Educators and librarians, for a variety of teaching tools, visit us at www.randomhouse.com/teachers

Library of Congress Cataloging-in-Publication Data
Cooney, Caroline B.
If the witness lied / Caroline B. Cooney.—1st ed.
p. cm.
Summary: Torn apart by tragedies and the publicity they brought, siblings Smithy, Jack, and Madison, aged fourteen to sixteen, tap into their parent's courage to pull together and protect their brother Tris, nearly three, from furthur media exploitation and a much more sinister threat.
ISBN 978-0-385-73448-6 (trade)—ISBN 978-0-385-90451-3 (Gibraltar lib. bdg.)—ISBN 978-0-375-89106-9 (e-book) [1. Brothers and sisters—Fiction. 2. Grief—Fiction. 3. Orphans—Fiction. 4. Celebrities—Fiction. 5. Family life—Connecticut—Fiction. 6. Reality television programs—Fiction. 7. Connecticut—Fiction.] I. Title.
PZ7.C7834If 2009
[Fic]—dc22
2008023959

The text of this book is set in 11-point Goudy.
Printed in the United States of America
10 9 8 7 6 5 4 3 2 1
First Edition

When I was in high school and people knew me as Kitty Bruce, I was a page at the Perrot Memorial Library in Old Greenwich, Connecticut. Many years later, my nephew Ransom Bruce was also a page there. I loved the library—the graceful curving white marble stairs, the wood-paneled children's room, the back stacks. I learned the Dewey decimal system, which was like a special language, and often when I recall some book from my childhood, I see its position on the shelves in the Perrot library. I've moved several times over the years, and I have used and enjoyed many libraries and admired many librarians, but there will always be a special place in my heart for my first love: the Perrot Memorial Library.

This book is dedicated to two of its wonderful librarians, whose early deaths are such a loss:
Kate McClelland and Kathy Krasniewicz

One

THE GOOD THING ABOUT FRIDAY IS—IT'S NOT THURSDAY. JACK
Fountain lived through Thursday, and nothing bad happened: no
cameras, no microphones.

Of course, nothing good happened either. Jack did not hear
from either of his sisters.

Their father's birthday—and Jack and Madison and Smithy
pretended it wasn't there; that November fifth was just another day.

And in fact, thinks Jack, walking into the high school cafeteria, it was just another day. Dead people don't have birthdays.

Around him, hundreds of kids are buying lunch, skipping
lunch or finding lunch partners. His goal is to be normal, although the Fountain family stopped being normal a long time
ago. Jack is considering his options when Diana Murray walks
past. "We need to talk," she murmurs.

This seems odd. How would Diana know about Dad's
birthday?

But Diana does not pause beside Jack. She keeps walking, moving casually out of the cafeteria and into the hall.

If Diana doesn't want anybody to overhear their conversation, then this is not about a birthday. This is about Jack's baby brother, Tris. Something else has gone wrong; something Jack hasn't planned for. Diana is on the Tris protection team. It's a small group. Usually a two-year-old has parents to protect him, but Tris is not that lucky. He has only his big brother and his babysitter.

Jack returns his brown plastic tray to the clean pile and strolls away, as if merely leaving the hot line for the salad and sandwich line. Then he drifts out of the cafeteria and down the hall, where Diana is leaning over the watercooler.

Because of Tris, Diana knows more about Jack than he wants her to. But then, the world knows more about Jack than he wants it to. His friends love to display their lives on video sites, but they get to choose what's out there. Jack doesn't.

The last few students with first lunch hurry past. Jack stands behind Diana, pretending to wait his turn for a drink of water. He braces himself for a Tris nightmare. He's trapped in his failure-to-breathe mode: a clenched, solid feeling, as if he's a different species, and will now function without oxygen.

Diana speaks so quietly that Jack has to bend down to hear. He's grown almost six inches this year, making him the tallest sophomore, as well as the best known. Jack is popular. It's partly because he is the one who stays, the one who gives up everything, including varsity, to take care of Tris. But mostly, it's because he's been on television.

Television hung out in his yard, focused on his face and

2

attended the funerals. Of all his classmates, only Diana grasps that television is a force in destroying his family, and even Diana tells Jack how adorable he is in that shot where he lifts up his baby brother and carries him home.

Jack's cheek touches the thick, curly black hair Diana never seems to brush or trim or even know about. Diana's voice barely makes it through her hair. "Tris was playing outside this morning, before your aunt Cheryl took him to day care. When he saw me, he raced over to say hi."

Jack imagines his brother's little legs pumping as he hurries over two front yards to the Murray house. It's a true escape, because Aunt Cheryl usually takes Tris straight from the breakfast table to the car seat.

"Your aunt Cheryl was looking really annoyed, so I hauled him back and put him in his car seat for her."

Why do girls have to give so much data? Jack manages to breathe a little, slow and stealthy, as though he's keeping his lungs a secret. A pinpoint headache sparkles behind his eyes, like a tiny firecracker going off.

"I distracted your aunt Cheryl by asking about her plans for the day. She starts talking in this hysterical voice about closets and clutter. She's going to clean out your bedroom and paint it, Jack. She knows you'll never say yes, so she's doing it before you can stop her."

Laughter bursts out where panic has been building. This isn't about Tris. It's about one of Aunt Cheryl's silly TV shows. She lives for programs where people paint their walls. When she turns on the TV—actually, she never turns it off—she isn't hoping for a good movie with a car chase. She wants to see the lid pried off a paint can. She wants to gaze upon the sewing of window treatments. Her life's dream is to be a guest on such a show. Or any show.

Jack straightens up, grinning and breathing normally. His headache vanishes as fast as a change in the weather. "So who are you, then?" he teases. "Diana Murray, secret agent for remodeling plans?"

Diana looks up soberly. "The afghan your mother knit you? Your aunt Cheryl doesn't like the colors. The tickets from when you and your dad went to the World Series? Your aunt Cheryl doesn't like the frame. Your closet? Stuffed with junk? Your aunt Cheryl wants to chuck it."

Aunt Cheryl will throw anything out, so Jack habitually checks the trash cans. But it has not occurred to him that she might invade his very own closet. He cannot let this happen. His most precious possessions are on the floor of that closet.

The headache comes back so savagely Jack feels as if his brain is being dragged on the pavement, like a broken muffler scraping under a car.

Back when it happened, Jack believed everything would be okay. After all, the ambulance came quickly; the police gathered. These were professionals in his driveway. Jack was reassured. When they agreed to let Jack go along to the hospital, he walked over to his father's Jeep, reached through the open door, and got the sunglasses and cell phone, lying as usual in the little well next to the parking brake. Dad will need these, Jack thought. He never travels without them.

But it turned out that Dad was traveling to another world, where he would not, in fact, need them. And since he wouldn't need his watch or wallet, either, the hospital turned these over to Jack as well.

Jack cannot bear to touch or even look at them. But neither can he bear to lose them. They're inside Dad's steel-toed work boots, stowed in the back of the closet, where they're safe but he won't have to think about them. (After it happened, not thinking became a family specialty. It's hard to say whether Jack or Smithy or Madison is best at it.)

It's eleven-twenty.

If Aunt Cheryl has started her project, she could already have taken a carload to the dump. Actually, there is no dump anymore. There's a transfer station, which is worse. At a dump, Jack could poke around and retrieve things. But at the transfer station, belowground, where open metal containers guarded by a sanitation crew are eventually hooked up to trucks and driven away, nobody's going to let Jack jump down inside to hunt for old boots.

He can't wait until school ends at three o'clock. But if he leaves now, he'll miss trig and maybe chemistry as well before he can get back. Jack never skips. Study is holding him together this year. You can count on study. It doesn't die on you.

However, if Aunt Cheryl is remodeling, it's not just the boots at risk, or those four little possessions that mattered so much when Dad was alive and not at all once he was dead. There are other traces of Dad. Like the shelves he built for Jack. Dad was impatient. He didn't measure carefully. The shelves are askew.

Jack uses them for stuff that doesn't slide, like sweaters. Aunt Cheryl will have a carpenter rip out the nails Dad hammered in and throw away the wood he cut and stained.

"Thanks," Jack says to Diana, although he wants to scream, "Why did you wait so long? Aunt Cheryl could have the second coat of paint on!" But he cannot yell at Diana. So many females in his life and each one beyond his reach.

Jack checks the amount of adult supervision out here in the hall. None.

He trots to the door that kids prop open when they go outside to eat. Like most high school doors, it's exit only—it shuts behind you, and locks. Then you have to circle the entire building and come in at the front. Totally annoying. But under these circumstances, maybe coming back doesn't matter. He lets the door slam behind him. It's not that chilly, but it's drizzling, so nobody is outside. He rounds the gymnasium wing at a run. It has few windows, so there is little chance that he will be observed. Observing Jack is something of a school hobby, although lately it's cooled down. He cannot do anything that might heat it up again.

He unlocks his bike from the rack and straps on his helmet, which he left hanging on the handlebars and is lucky nobody stole. On the other hand, everybody knows which bike is Jack's: the one with the child seat. Celebrities get a pass.

The quickest route home is a shortcut over the soggy playing fields. His tires sink. It's slow going. A low chain-link fence divides the playing fields from the houses and streets beyond. Jack lifts his bike over the fence. Using a post as a pivot point, he vaults over with room to spare. It's a good feeling, as if he'll be able to vault over anything else in his path.

Probably not.

Now that he's on pavement, he can pedal fast. He's not sure what he plans to achieve once he gets home, other than rescuing the boots. The best plan is probably to slip in and out without Aunt Cheryl detecting him, which may be easy, since she will be in her usual position in front of the television and won't hear him. If they do meet, he's got to hang on to his temper.

Aunt Cheryl likes to tell people that Jack is so tall now, he's threatening; Jack looms over her; she cannot predict his behavior. Jack believes Cheryl Rand is preparing a case to present to the judge. Aunt Cheryl loves having Madison and Smithy out of the house. If she can arrange things so that Jack is gone too, how nice that will be. Once (only once, but it's tattooed on his heart) Tris had a classic meltdown, the kind of tantrum where you remind yourself not to have children of your own, and Cheryl said casually that Tris ought to be in foster care.

Foster care. Strangers bringing up his brother. Authorities taking Tris to some address they won't even tell Jack.

It would kill his mother. She planned so carefully how things would go.

Every day—certainly today—Jack yearns to yell at Cheryl. Throw something at her, preferably something with sharp edges. At least do a little swearing. But that would give her ammunition.

Jack takes another shortcut through a neighbor's deep property. The neighbor hates this, but the neighbor is at work. There is no fence between Jack's backyard on Chesmore and this one on Kensington. Instead, the backyards are divided by a seasonal brook, whose banks are thick with trees and brush. Jack follows the path he and his father created in another life. He passes the tiny dam he and Tris built, and the tiny pond where he takes Tris "fishing."

Bit by bit, Aunt Cheryl has been removing every trace of Jack's mother and father from the house. Jack stores his rescues in the garage attic, a space reached by unfolding a heavy wooden staircase. Aunt Cheryl might not even know that there *is* an attic. For a woman consumed by how a house looks, she is amazingly unaware of how a house works. Jack removed the cord used to pull the stairs down and replaced it with an almost invisible knob. In the poor lighting of the garage, now that the telltale cord is gone, it's unlikely she will ever realize there's storage up there.

Jack decides to transfer the boots to the garage attic. Once they're safely hidden, he can tackle Aunt Cheryl about leaving his bedroom alone.

Emerging from the little woods, Jack can make out a car in his driveway. It isn't Aunt Cheryl's. She keeps hers in the garage. She hates weather. Hot or cold, sunny or snowing, she doesn't want to be out in it. Jack has never known her to exercise. Her only walk is from the kitchen through the breezeway and into the garage. Once in her car, she uses the automatic garage door opener. She has no use for fresh air. It's an ongoing problem, because Tris, if trapped inside on a nice day, spends his time drumming on locked doors, or maybe kicking them, trying to break out.

Jack approaches his house at an angle so that the garage blocks anybody indoors from seeing him. Leaning his bike against the back of the garage, he lets himself into the breezeway, a funny little glass room with closets and recycling bins at one end and the kitchen door at the other. When his mother was alive, this space was thick with geraniums, and you walked through a moist jungle of green and red.

The visitor's car, an indigo-blue BMW convertible, is parked right on the other side of the glass. Nice car if the sun shines. Not what Jack pictures for a housepainter. Do decorators make that much money? Or does Aunt Cheryl have guests? Jack would have said that Cheryl Rand had no friends, but for all he knows, she's president of the Newcomers Club and drivers of spiffy new BMWs drop in all the time.

The good news is she'll be busy with the guest. And they will be near the TV, because Aunt Cheryl is always near the TV. She doesn't turn it off for anybody.

Quietly, he opens the door to the kitchen and eases inside.

He can hear the television, which is good. She's occupied. He walks carefully to the carpeted center hall. No signs of decorating. No drop cloths, ladders, or shifted furniture. No smell of paint. He's a little vulnerable here because a wide archway opens into the living room, but the sofa and chairs are at the far end, facing the TV, which is wall-mounted above the fireplace. Aunt Cheryl lives on that side of the room.

Jack goes up the stairs in a flash, tiptoeing past his sisters' rooms.

When their father died, Jack was left with two priorities: take care of Tris; do well in school. All else fell away. Whenever he lets himself think about the day when everything went dark, pain takes over. It has overtaken his sister Smithy. It has overtaken his sister Madison. Jack cannot let it happen to him. He is Tris's only hope.

He steps into his own bedroom. Untouched. The relief is huge.

In his closet, Jack silently moves sneakers, sandals and miscellaneous junk until he reaches Dad's work boots. He thrusts a hand inside each one and feels around. Sunglasses and wallet still in the left boot, cell phone and watch safe in the right boot.

It dawns on him that since Aunt Cheryl is home, her car is parked beneath the folding stair. He has no access to the garage attic. He'll have to take the boots to Diana's. Mrs. Murray is always home, sitting at her computer. She books moving vans, sending full and partial loads all over the country. Whenever Jack comes over, she hops up and fixes him a hot snack. Mrs. Murray disapproves of cold food. It isn't filling, she says, frowning. Her specialty is a ham and cheese sandwich where she butters the bread on the outside and then squashes the sandwich in a special waffle iron. It comes out crusted and toasty, drippy with cheese.

Jack's mother loved to bake. Mainly cookies, but sometimes she surprised them with a chocolate cream pie or a jelly roll.

Aunt Cheryl watches cooking shows and has favorite chefs, but she does not cook. She heats. Jack and Tris are fed like pets left behind while the owners go on vacation—enough kibble to graze on and a bowl of water.

It's one of a thousand ways in which Jack envies his sisters. Real food.

Madison and Smithy communicate now and then, usually by e-mail: stuff they could write to anybody. Jack feels like an army private in a war zone, desperate to be told that his sacrifice matters—but the only mail he gets is from kindly strangers addressed to Dear Soldier.

They don't phone each other. If they hear each other's voices, they are out of things to say before they start.

If only Mrs. Murray had agreed to take Smithy in! His younger sister would be two houses away. They could have worked things out. They—

But Jack has a rule. Never consider what could have, would have, should have happened. Because it didn't.

Jack grabs an old backpack, slides the boots in, buckles it closed, but cannot get it on. He's much wider in the shoulders since he last wore it. Opening the straps as far as possible, he wriggles his arms into them and heads for the stairs.

The TV seems louder than usual. A rich rolling voice fills the lower floor. A public voice, proud of itself.

Jack pauses on the fourth step from the bottom. It isn't the TV. It's live. It's the visitor.

"You are absolutely right, Cheryl," booms the voice, deep and masculine. "We're so glad you called us. The situation in this house is riveting. Perfect for television."

Has Aunt Cheryl's dream come true? A room in this house will be featured on some TV decorating show? Aunt Cheryl would definitely babble hysterically to Diana if that was about to happen.

"So much tragedy and emotion!" cries the man, as if he lives for tragedy and emotion.

Jack sits on the stair. He doesn't mean to. His knees stop holding him. There is no tragedy and no emotion in wall color. This is not about painting bedrooms. This is about Tris.

Now, when Jack needs stealthy breathing, his lungs wheeze. The sparkly headache evolves, as if he's going to have seizures.

The speaker is pumped. "I love it, Cheryl! We'll line up the neighbors. We'll film little Tristan in day care. We'll interview his little classmates and their parents."

Jack has dealt with television. It's not a friend. It has a job: to provide entertainment. It has chosen Tris before. He's photogenic. Last year when they filmed Tris, they found him so adorable. Such a little angel, they cried, and look what he did.

"And of course we'll want to film the older brother for several days. I love the way he's standing firm and being loyal. We'll follow him in school."

Jack is "the older brother."

Followed? For several days? In school? Where he can still find safety in science and math? Where people have almost forgotten what happened?

Can they do this without Jack's permission?

12

The voice is really into it now. "The sisters are the real drama. I love how they refuse to be under the same roof. Wonderful theater."

Theater. Where you pay money to stare.

"We'll get a huge audience. Advertisers will sign up in a heartbeat. I see it as a three- or four-part docudrama."

There's a new sound. Jack hasn't heard it often, but he recognizes it. Aunt Cheryl is giggling with delight.

She has sold Tris to television.

Two

MADISON FOUNTAIN HAS SKIPPED SCHOOL AND IS FAKING ILLNESS so she can spend Friday on the Emmers' sofa, watching television. She's alone, of course, because Mr. and Mrs. Emmer are at work and Henry and Kimmy are at school. Madison rotates through every channel the Emmers get, which is a lot. She wants something to take her mind off yesterday. She tries weather, sports, a soap opera, cartoons and music videos, but she can't stay on anything. She finds herself clicking madly at the remote, as if an Up or a Down will blot out her thoughts.

Madison is tightly wrapped in a blanket. Back Before, Madison's mother knit all the time, churning out socks and sweaters, blankets and afghans. Laura Fountain loved to knit. She'd have knit furniture if she could've figured out how. But when Madison moved in with the Emmers, she did not bring a single thing knit by her mother. She holds her mother responsible. It isn't fair, but she can't dislodge the belief.

Deep inside the blanket, Madison lets herself think about

yesterday. Not just any Thursday, although only three people know this, and Madison chose not to contact the other two.

Mrs. Emmer always takes Thursday afternoons off, because she works on Saturdays. Yesterday, she picked the three children up after school and headed to the mall. Kimmy needed dance shoes and Henry needed a long-sleeved white shirt with a collar and cuffs for the chorus concert.

Madison sat there like baggage. The Emmers are sick of her. At first it was You poor baby, crushed by fate. Why don't you stay with us until things settle down?

And now it's like—She's still here? She hasn't left yet?

Of course they don't say it out loud. They're nice people. That's why they're her godparents.

Back Before, Madison's mother liked to watch films of her children. There's a nice one of Madison at eight weeks, beautiful in a lacy white gown with pink satin ribbons, sleeping through her christening. Off to the side stand the Emmers, watching a ceremony that means nothing to them, because they don't go to church. But they love the concept of being godparents. They're all dressed up and promising before God and the congregation to rear baby Madison in the Christian faith.

In fact, the Emmers are relieved that Madison hasn't done anything difficult like mention church. They're off the hook, godparent-wise. They can give her supper and a bedroom and they're done.

Madison knows she's being mean.

Mr. and Mrs. Emmer are wonderful. Henry and Kimmy are fun and cheerful. Madison fits right into her new school, and if

15

anybody in this town has heard of the Fountain family, they don't say so. Madison escapes notice. Hers is a popular name, and among so many other Madisons, she blends into the crowd.

When she moved to the Emmer house, Madison didn't even bring photographs. If she needs to see what her real family looks like—*looked* like—she can go online to the site where her parents stored their photographs. She never does. Month after month, Madison Fountain holds herself still, not remembering her parents and not thinking about her sister and brothers.

But on Thursday there was no blocking out memory. November fifth was her father's birthday. On the way to the mall, Madison slid into last year, when her father turned forty. She could almost taste the birthday cake. It was chocolate, of course; Dad loved chocolate. They had ordered the largest sheet cake and specified white icing, because writing shows up best against white. They took turns printing with little gel tubes. Last year it had been Smithy's turn to write first. First was a bad position, because everybody wrote on top of you. But Smithy got to choose the best color. She went with red, and wrote I LV U DAD.

Madison thought about that a lot. Smithy abbreviated "love."

Mrs. Emmer pulled into the vast mall parking lot. Madison just wanted to be alone with the rare treat of memories and light a mental candle for Dad. "I'll stay in the car and do homework," she said.

The sun was shining, and with the temperature in the fifties, the interior of the car would get toasty. Madison couldn't wait for the Emmers to go, and they must have felt the same, because they vaulted out. "Give me an hour!" cried Madison, turning her head so she wouldn't see how glad they were to be a real family, without the interloper. Her eyes swung over a horizon of parked cars.

Her father's Jeep was one of them.

• • •

Every Friday morning at Smith Fountain's boarding school, there is an eight-thirty assembly before classes begin.

On this Friday morning, Dr. Dresser, the headmistress, is less dull than usual. She is explaining the mechanics of getting four hundred kids home for Thanksgiving and Christmas. Almost everyone loves boarding school. It's so much fun—always busy and demanding and special. But it isn't home, and now home looks like a treat—a present with ribbons—and everybody gets one.

Everybody except Smithy.

Last winter, Smithy applied on her own to a boarding school she located online, and this initiative worked in her favor; the school was impressed. Not many fourteen-year-old girls pull off applications without parents. Smithy was accepted for the second semester of freshman year—the only student among four hundred who is truly without parents. In fact, many kids have multiple parents, from remarriages and ex-stepparents who stay in touch. There is a boy in Smithy's biology class who has seven active parents.

Her classmates come from all over the United States. They do not ask about her family situation because it does not occur to them that she has one. They are, however, interested in her first name.

Before she got married, my mother's last name was Smith, she explains. Boring and ordinary for a last name, but interesting for a first name.

Smithy's roommate is envious because her name is Kate, and she even looks like some of the other Kates and Katies in the school, whereas nobody else is named Smith.

Kate has never met an orphan. It's so romantic! Not having parents—how exciting! It reminds Kate of her favorite childhood book, *Anne of Green Gables*. Kate seems to visualize life for orphans as a series of sunny adventures. She's eager to bring Smithy home and show her off.

Smithy is eager to go. What a bonus—she doesn't even have to show up at her real home for vacations.

Smithy gets used to dorm life among eighty girls, half of whom she likes. The girls share rooms, snacks, homework, conversation and shampoo. As if living in a tiny castle in the Middle Ages, they have no privacy at any time. With so many girls, so much talk, and the constant schedule of activities, Smithy can pretend that Back Before doesn't exist.

She now has a life without shopping and, in fact, without a town: the school is in the middle of nowhere. A life with mandatory study hours six evenings a week, and mandatory sports, so she will have a healthy body as well as a healthy mind. A life that after ten p.m. is one long slumber party, as long as they don't wake the dorm proctor.

It occurs to Smithy, as she sits not listening to Dr. Dresser, that her escape from home worked because she pulled it off during easy months. February, March, April, May—who cares? Nothing happens then anyway. As for last summer, she spent ten days with Kate's family and then returned to boarding school for summer session, much more fun than it sounds. Hot, sweaty weeks full of classes and picnics, softball and ballroom dancing, storytelling competitions and a build-your-own-radio contest.

One weekend her grandparents showed up. Dad's parents, her Fountain grandparents. Smithy was almost angry at Nonny and Poppy for reminding her that she had a family out there whether she liked it or not. She managed to be exceptionally busy. Her grandparents ended up talking mostly to Kate.

Because of the assembly, Smithy can be sure it's Friday, and that means she can be sure Thursday is over. Dad's birthday. Gone.

I didn't call Jack, thinks Smithy. I didn't call Madison. I didn't treat Daddy's birthday differently from any other day.

Their father would have been forty-one. Last year Smithy was the first cake writer. Tris went second, and chose blue, and they steered his little fist so he wouldn't totally mess up the frosting. Jack wrote GO DAD in yellow, and ran out of gel before he finished LOVE JACK. Madison got to go last. She printed HAPPY BDAY in green and had enough left to finish JACK.

"Anyone not going home for the holidays must come to me for alternative arrangements," says Dr. Dresser.

Only Smithy and the kids from distant countries like Japan or India will need alternative arrangements.

Home.

Her two brothers still live there. One brother is a saint, and the other—well, what do you call Tris?

And does it matter?

* * *

Madison cannot distract herself with television. Her mind reenters Thursday in the parking lot. She's getting out of the Emmers' car, walking unsteadily toward the Jeep. It's over one row, but far to the rear of the lot, alone on the flat pavement. She's afraid of it.

A drum set begins playing in her head. Wooden sticks snap against her skull. It's the tuneless headache she gets whenever she thinks of this moment.

After it happened, Dad's car got towed, but where to? Who kept it? Madison never asked. She certainly didn't want to see it again. Almost certainly, she isn't seeing it now, either. Jeeps are popular. Just because this is the same model, year and color as Dad's does not make it Dad's.

The Jeep isn't locked. Jeep owners are not big on locking.

Madison wrenches her eyes from the steering wheel, in case she hallucinates that her father is sitting there for the last time. She detours around the Jeep to peer through the passenger door instead.

Dad had a habit shared by nobody. He carved his initials on

everything. He carved RF onto the wood surfaces of his desk and the picnic table, into the leather of his beloved work boots. (Dad had an office job, so he liked to get down and dirty on weekends.) He carved RF + LF into the maple tree that shades the backyard.

He scratched RF into the dashboard of his Jeep.

That will ruin its resale value, people used to say, disapproving.

"I have four children to support," Dad would answer, laughing. "I'll be driving this until my kids are out of college."

No, thinks Madison. You won't.

Even with her nose against the window, she can't see if anything's carved on the dash.

Do people still have birthdays when they're dead? While the Emmers are in the department store, should Madison run into the card shop to buy a card? A funny one, because Daddy liked to laugh. Last year they were laughing over the cake until Madison finished JACK and they realized that Mom would not be adding her own I LOVE YOU in the final, least desirable color. They piled onto the old sofa, weeping for Mom.

Except Tris. For Tris, Mommy is a photograph.

Madison finds herself opening the passenger door of the Jeep. Automatically she does what people do when they open a car door: she gets in and sits down. What if the owner comes? Oh, sorry, just replaying my father's death.

In the cup holders and the little well where Dad always left his cell phone, sunglasses and loose change, the stranger keeps garbage: an empty coffee cup, a crumpled napkin.

Glare from the sunlight makes it difficult to see the dashboard.

21

Madison leans forward to search for initials, steadying herself on the parking brake.

The driver has set the brake. Reflex, probably, since no brake is needed on a flat parking lot. The Fountain driveway, on the other hand, slopes. A car left in Madison's driveway must be in gear, and the parking brake must be on, or the car will roll backward.

After all this time of not letting herself remember, not letting herself picture this, not letting herself go there in any way, Madison is here. She is here so completely that her hand is actually on the very brake that ended it all.

Tris would have been in his car seat, which was so big it barely fit in the back. Tris had to cooperate when it was time to be strapped in, holding his arms just right, although he'd rather have done everything by himself. He had only just turned two, and was not strong enough to latch the belts.

A funny coldness wafts through Madison's head.

Tris wasn't strong enough to fasten the plastic snaps of his own little restraint system. Then how could he be strong enough—

She shakes herself. What Tris did was *unfasten* his restraints. Always easier.

Dad got out of the Jeep to check something. They'll never know what. He left the motor running, put the Jeep in neutral and yanked up the parking brake. He planned to get right back in.

Tris probably wanted to see what Daddy was doing. He was probably proud of himself, wiggling out from under the webs and straps, climbing up front. He loved the front. All those gadgets and dials. All the important stuff. And of course, Daddy sat in front. Tris always wanted to be with Daddy.

When it happened, Madison was the first one out of the house. Well, except for Aunt Cheryl. The loudest noise came from Cheryl, but Tris was also screaming. Tris was standing on this very seat. In his little hands, he clasped Dad's cell phone. (Tris got his hands on somebody's phone and was totally happy. From the time he was twelve months old, Tris thumbed a phone exactly the way his father did, holding it up to his face at the same angle, squinching his eyebrows before he answered, just like Daddy, and most of all, taking pictures, just like Daddy.)

In his hands? thinks Madison now. Both hands? But then— how did he—?

Tris must have released the parking brake first and then picked up the phone. And because Tris had somehow locked himself in, Cheryl had started beating on the car door and screaming at him. No wonder Tris panicked.

Yet how odd that with Dad's cell phone, sunglasses and change sitting right there—Dad always left them right there—Tris played with the brake at all. It's just a stick, whereas cell phones are joy, sunglasses are grown-up and coins are fun.

A queer, cold thought is surfacing in Madison's mind, like a predator coming out of the water. She tugs the stranger's parking brake. It does not release.

She shifts her weight and tries a second time. It does not release.

When it happened, Tris was two and he weighed twenty-five

pounds. If Madison is having trouble, and she's nearly seventeen and a hundred and ten pounds, then . . . ?

Madison puts a little muscle into it. The brake releases.

The Jeep, of course, does not move, because the parking lot has no tilt. Madison is almost fainting, but she remembers to check the dash. No initials. Of course there aren't initials. She's invading somebody else's car. She resets the brake, opens the door and gets out.

A possibility is filling her head. The thought swells until it pushes against her eyes and she bulges with it.

She backs away, as if the stranger's Jeep will attack.

But it is knowledge—or at least a good guess—that is attacking Madison Fountain.

Don't be silly, she tells herself. Any given Jeep is bound to be different from the next one. Just because this one has a stiff brake doesn't mean Dad's did.

Madison makes it to the Emmers' car. Falls in. Tries to warm herself in the bottled sun.

"Look what I got!" shrieks Kimmy Emmer.

Madison almost has a heart attack. She manages to exclaim over the wisdom and style of Kimmy's purchase. She participates in conversation. It is decided that they will have Chinese take-out for dinner.

All the way back to the Emmers' on Thursday, Madison reminds herself that there was a witness to the accident. They know what happened: the witness told them.

Now, Friday morning, in the stuffy dark of the blanket, Madison allows the swollen thought to come all the way out.

24

If Tris would not release the brake . . . but the brake *was* released . . . then somebody else released it.

The witness lied.

· · ·

Dr. Dresser dismisses the assembly. Kate bubbles with excitement. "We usually have about twenty people for Thanksgiving," she tells Smithy. "Grandma and Grandpa fly in from Michigan, and then my cousins, the ones in Pennsylvania."

Smithy will share the cousins, because Kate will be Smithy's "alternative arrangements."

Thanks to Kate and summer school, the only stretch during which Smithy had to live in her own house was a week last summer, just before fall semester began. All those August days dripped with anxiety as well as sweat.

Nothing was what she had pictured.

Tris, who'd barely talked when Smithy left in February, now rattled off whole paragraphs. He had opinions on television cartoons, demanded to be driven over to check the progress at his favorite construction site, bragged about his swimming technique and refused to eat ice cream in a cup. "I'm big now! I can have a cone!"

Tris had to be told who Smithy is. "You're in my scrapbook!" he said excitedly, hurrying to get the precious album, so carefully put together by their mother: a biography of Mom; Dad; Madison, the oldest; Jack, the middle; and Smithy, the youngest; right up to the birth of Tris.

Smithy was unnerved by the welcome her baby brother had given her. "He's glad to see me," she said to Jack.

Her brother shrugged. "I tell him how much you miss him."

So Jack was not just a good guy. He was a good enough guy to make up for his sisters.

(After that, Smithy could hardly even look at Jack. But because her older brother had grown almost half a foot, she was aware of him every moment. She imagined him going weekly to the mall for larger clothing. She wanted to talk about school but couldn't. Although Jack is a year older, they're in the same grade. When he was entering first, Jack tested so poorly, he was kept back. It's a family joke, because Jack has turned out to be by far the smartest.)

Tris scrambled into Smithy's lap and settled in to read his album to her. "And this is the trip to Missouri to Nonny and Poppy's," he said. "I'm not born yet. Here's where Daddy drives over the Mississippi River." He mangled the word "Mississippi" and Jack helped him. "Everybody gets out! Here's Mommy! Here's Smithy! It's you, Smithy!"

How unfamiliar his weight was in her lap.

How amazing that he could be comfortable there.

When it happened, Smithy had raced back into the house for the spare keys, fumbling through kitchen drawers. It took a nightmarishly long time to find them. A neighbor snatched the keys from her hand, unlocked the Jeep and drove it off Dad, while Smithy lifted Tris from the front seat, where he was sobbing. Only then did Smithy make out the words Cheryl was screaming: "He did it! Tris did it! Tris released the brake! Tris killed his own father!"

Smithy set Tris down. She never picked him up again.

That week in August, Tris couldn't get enough of this exciting big sister. He tagged along after her with the dedication of an undercover cop.

Madison came over for a few meals, and once for the whole day, but mostly she stayed with the Emmers, using her old home as a storage closet.

Madison, Jack and Smithy didn't talk. They just waited it out.

When Smithy had left last winter, Aunt Cheryl was still using the downstairs guest room, but by August, she'd moved into the master bedroom upstairs. It was okay for Cheryl to use Mom's dishes, but it was not okay for her to use Mom's closet. Smithy kept wondering about the stuff. Who cleaned it out? Where was it now? A thrift shop? The dump? A tag sale? She could not bring herself to ask. She didn't want to hear Jack say that he had handled it, and his sisters should have been here to help.

The week in August was slow and airless. At last, it was time for Madison to drive Smithy to the train station. In Boston, the school van would pick her up.

"Bye!" cried Tris, waving happily. He is the only Fountain child who does not know that some good-byes are forever.

"Good-bye," said Jack politely. He looked confused, as if he could not remember where they had met.

Aunt Cheryl was watching television. She didn't come out to say good-bye and Smithy didn't go in. Cheryl seemed more like furniture than an aunt.

On the way to the station, the sisters didn't talk of important things. They're the ones who left. They're glad and they're horrified.

Instead Madison talked about her car, a mildly sporty four-year-old silver Celica.

There's a trust fund for the children, from their parents' life insurance and investments. A trustee named Wade handles this. Wade pays for Smithy's boarding school and shells out for Madison's used car. Smithy had almost forgotten about cars. At a boarding school, you walk.

The drive to the train station was swift. Smithy wanted to cry, Let's just keep going, Madison! Let's drive away! Let's start over!

But she *has* started over. In another state. In another world, actually.

When the train came in, Madison hugged her younger sister. "I love you, Smithy. Somehow . . ."

Somehow what? It'll be all right? It won't be all right, and they know it.

Smithy was grateful for the train that took her away. A boarding school is designed to keep students too busy to get homesick. Smithy hadn't given her family a thought until yesterday. Dad's birthday.

Thinking about Dad is the hardest thing in the whole world. Except for thinking about Mom. And now Dr. Dresser brings up the tough months: the months with Thanksgiving and Christmas. Thanksgiving for home; Christmas for love. The two things Smithy has abandoned.

Kate talks of Thanksgiving food. Of mashed potatoes and pumpkin pie.

I have to go home, thinks Smithy.

And then, rushing over her, strong as tides or gales, is miraculous knowledge. She *wants* to go home.

• • •

Jack cannot feel a heartbeat in his own chest. His lungs are not inflating. His eyes are not blinking.

On the other side of the wall, the television still murmuring beside her, Aunt Cheryl's voice rises with excitement. "When do we start?"

"The anniversaries are coming up. We have to capitalize on that."

So the media never even knew about Dad's birthday. All Jack's anxiety yesterday was pointless. This man means the day Laura Fountain died for her child and the day Reed Fountain died because of that child. They are both winter days, cold days that get dark early.

Jack's body has begun to tremble, like one of those old, old people with thin white hair and spots on the back of their hands who sit silently shuddering to themselves.

"We should start filming immediately. And there's the nice coincidence of Tris's third birthday. Are you planning a big party? Do you have a theme?" The man chuckles. "Patricide?" he says. "No, no, just kidding."

But he is not kidding.

Tris will be frozen in time. Frozen, with his crime in his little hand. There will be no escape. Not now. Not next year. Not when Tris is a teenager or a grown-up. He will be a piece of television, dragged out whenever they need a shocking example.

Back when Mom made her fatal decision, the world grabbed hold of it. Jack never figured out how that happened. Overnight she was the flashpoint of a controversy. There were networks and media all over the place. They parked in the yard, they rapped on the door, they phoned, they filmed. Against their will, the Fountain family was on national television and in national magazines, the subject of blogs and editorials and talk shows.

At school, Jack was regarded with envy. His classmates saw glamour and the possibility of fame.

Jack struggles to breathe. Thinking this through will require oxygen.

The producer in his living room will love it if Jack charges in, protesting and yelling. The guy probably travels with a mini-cam so he can snatch up chance encounters and add them to his arsenal.

Because this is war. A battle waged against a three-year-old.

And the Tris protection team is small and weak.

Three

KATE DANCES ALONGSIDE SMITHY. KATE'S BODY IS ALWAYS BUSY. She taps, leaps, turns, whirls. She's the ballerina inside the jewelry box, always wound up.

Kate and Smithy are a good pair, the way Smithy once was with Diana Murray. Madison is the sister who is Diana's age, but Smithy is the sister who became Diana's best friend. Smithy spent her life racing across yards, pounding up the wooden steps of the Murrays' back deck and in the back door, shouting hello to Mrs. Murray, eternally at her computer, and racing up to Diana's room.

Smithy has never mentioned Diana to Kate.

"Second breakfast?" asks her roommate. Kate is as thin as a bookmark, but always consumes a double breakfast. At her first breakfast, she has a glass of orange juice and toast with peanut butter. Now she will have cold cereal. She will spend an amazing amount of time studying the cereal choices.

Smithy finds herself stranded in front of shiny many-slice

toasters in which she is not toasting anything, because she can't remember how toast happens.

The thought of Christmas brings music, carols that chime in her heart. "Joy to the world." Oh, sure, Smithy laughs and tells jokes and is good company for Kate. But joy? No.

How vividly Smithy remembers Christmas Eve, when being in the dorky children's choir is finally worth it—the long robes, the procession down the aisle with a real candle, the flame shivering in its glass cup, the organ pipes making the pews tremble with the huge D-major chords of "Joy to the World."

Smithy has spent a long time being mad. Mad at cancer, gravity, Tris, Mom, Dad and God. She often tells God what a loser he is for killing her parents and destroying her life. Smithy still can't believe it. This is not the Dark Ages, where your parents go and get the Black Death and you're orphaned.

Somehow Smithy is having an English muffin with butter and thick plum jam.

"I'm off to algebra!" cries Kate. "See you later!" She dances away, slender and shiny as a twirling baton.

Smithy sets the muffin down. She understands at last. She isn't mad at Mom or Dad. She isn't mad at Tris or God. She's mad at herself.

Whatever else Tristan Reed Fountain is, he is Smithy's brother. Smithy's mother gave her life for this baby, and Smithy promised to honor that.

She didn't.

Smithy would have said that hers is the most complex situation in the whole wide world. But that isn't so. Her situation is simple. To have her family back, to have Thanksgiving and Christmas back, to do something right for a change, all she has to do is go home.

• • •

Jack is immobilized on the stairs. He feels tacked there, like the carpet he's sitting on.

"We'll want the sisters here for Tris's birthday party," says the rolling voice. "Film them in their own house, where it happened. Where they have to admit the truth. So first let's get the sisters home."

"Smith is at boarding school, so she's easy," says Aunt Cheryl. "I'll call the administration and feed them a line. I'm sure they'll agree with, say, court-ordered family therapy. As for Madison, she's living with friends of her father's, a dozen miles from here. They'll bring Madison right over. They've been talking to the trustee anyhow about how to get Madison out of their house."

"Excellent. We'll bring in a psychiatrist. I know just the person. We've worked with him before, and he's good at coaxing out hidden emotions."

Jack is dragged now and then to a school counselor who likes to say that Jack has lost touch with his emotions. She's nuts. Jack has so many emotions they gallop around night and day. They've made ruts in his brain. He sees his emotions coming and he ducks.

"The best footage," says the man, "will be at the day-care center, filming this little boy who looks so normal as he plays among children who really *are* normal. A voice-over will explain that this child, in fact, killed both his mother and his father."

Cancer killed Mom, Jack wants to explain. An accident killed Dad.

But what's the fun in that? TV has to entertain. It can't be bothered with details.

Aunt Cheryl is so excited she's clapping. "I haven't talked to the day-care director yet. Maybe you should call her. I'm sure you'd do it better. After all, an associate producer? It's so official. Especially if we show up with a camera crew. Is the crew on the way? And the parents of the other children—do they have to sign off, or whatever?"

"Every parent wants their kid on television. I'm not worried about that. Any chance we can drop in on the day care today?"

This man is about to start filming and Jack is hanging out on the stairs, tugging at carpet shreds? Worrying about whether he's breathing too loudly?

Jack is on his feet. He tiptoes, yet flies, through the hall, into the kitchen, out the breezeway, onto the grass. He's on his bike, bumping over the curb, pedaling hard. The backpack confuses him. He doesn't often wear one.

The day-care center is a few miles west. Jack takes a shortcut he rarely uses, because the yard is home to an unfriendly Lab. Usually there's no such thing, but this dog is a biter. Jack knows how the dog feels. He would love to sink his teeth into the trespasser at his house. He goes through the dog's yard so fast he figures a cheetah couldn't catch him.

They can film all the day care they want.

But they are not filming Tris.

* * *

Madison flings off the blanket and gets down to the business of finding some decent TV. Grimly, she pauses at every channel.

She is startled to find her former church on the local-access cable channel. The banner explains that each Sunday service is broadcast three times the following week. Who knew?

The camera is positioned high in the second-floor gallery, at the rear. Even from behind, Madison recognizes some of the congregation: parents of her old friends or friends of her parents. The Fountains used to sit on the left, halfway back. After Mom died, Dad couldn't seem to organize himself to get everybody to church. There's something about Sunday morning that just takes more time, especially if you have to dress a baby. Church slipped away.

On television, little kids scurry forward to sit on the chancel steps for the children's sermon. When she was little, Madison used to feel so important up there. She used to love church. An hour in which to think of good things. But this year good things are hard to find in the Fountain family.

Aunt Cheryl isn't interested in church, so it's no surprise that Tris isn't among the children. Jack probably doesn't go on his own. Who wants to go alone? Madison certainly doesn't.

The children sing "Jesus Loves Me."

A few months before Tris was born, when Mom could still sing (at the end, she didn't have enough breath), she made a CD. She recorded game songs like "I'm a little teapot, short and stout," and children's hymns, including "Jesus Loves Me," and read favorite picture books, so that her fourth child would hear his mother's voice. Every night, Dad played that CD for Tris to fall asleep to. Madison couldn't stand the CD. Her mother's voice but not her presence? It was like an endless broken promise. She never asked Dad how he felt. There are a thousand things it's too late to ask now.

"Today in Sunday school," says the minister—it's Reverend Phillips, who christened Madison—"you'll learn about Ruth. Ruth has her own book in the Bible. It's only four pages long. How many pages long are the books *you* read?"

"I read chapter books now!" shouts a little girl.

"I can't read yet," says a little boy, worried.

"But we all love books," says Reverend Phillips. "Ruth's story is about loyalty. Does anybody know what that word means? If you're loyal, what kind of things do you do?"

If there is anybody who has failed the loyalty test, it is Madison Fountain. She turns off the television before she has to hear more about Ruth, who probably does everything right, as opposed to Madison herself, who has definitely done everything wrong. Madison, the one who runs when the going gets tough.

Madison is no longer faking it. She really is sick. In the kitchen she considers the can of chunky chicken rice soup Mrs. Emmer has left on the counter. Her own mother did not give her soup when she was sick. Laura Fountain's theory was, who ever wanted chicken broth? Here. Have a cookie, hot from the oven. And Mom was never sick herself, so she had little sympathy for people who were. She'd yell, "Go to bed! Sleep it off! If you're going to throw up, don't miss the toilet!"

Madison still cannot fathom how her mother got cancer. Laura Fountain always seems like the wrong person to have died young. All that energy and noise and song. All those projects and laughter. How did cancer get past those defenses?

It's almost lunchtime. Madison is still in her pajamas. Even when Mom was dying and things were awful and promised to get more awful, no matter what, Mom got up, got dressed, fixed her hair, or had somebody else fix it when she was too weak, and put on makeup. "Always be ready to face the world," said Laura Fountain. "Never stay in bed whimpering."

All these months, has Madison essentially stayed in bed whimpering?

The feel of that parking brake is still in the palm of Madison's hand. Her fingers curl around it. Her thumb finds the tip.

What really happened that day in the Jeep?

Madison is disgusted with herself. Is she going to be one of those pathetic creatures who sees a conspiracy in everything? The police must have tested Dad's Jeep. They must have towed it to their lab, fingerprinted it, run tests and concluded that it was an accident. They must have questioned the one and only witness and decided she was telling the truth.

No. Madison cannot barrel into her old house and accuse Cheryl Rand of murder.

It's because of Daddy's birthday, she tells herself. I got all emotional and sentimental on Thursday. I wanted a way out. Well, there isn't one.

In the room she shares with Kimmy Emmer, Madison dresses carefully, like her mother, taking into consideration weather, fabric, color, fashion and utility.

Now she is all dressed up with nowhere to go.

Maybe she'll drive over to her house anyway.

For once, the road home is not blocked by rage or despair. In fact, today looks pretty safe. All four Emmers are at work or at school. Jack is at school. Tris is at day care.

Cheryl is a woman of few interests: she will be watching TV or she'll be out shopping.

"Cheryl" is a soft, round, pleasant name. "Cheryl" sounds like a person who listens to classic rock, irons aprons and plays bunko. In fact, she's not an aunt at all. She's a glorified housekeeper.

In Aunt Cheryl's case, that word is literal: she wants the house and she wants to keep it. Once she's in charge, she inches through the rooms, gaining control of a corner here and a bit of wall space there, making it her own. Madison figures that by now Jack is down to a few square feet of old carpet.

What will Jack think if Madison shoulders her way back into his life? Jack has a great heart. The few times they've talked on the phone, he hasn't sounded angry. He's never said how hard it is for him. On the other hand, he's never asked her to come back.

Reminding herself that she can change her mind, she packs a bag. It's just pajamas, a toothbrush and a change of clothing; it doesn't mean anything. She'll toss it on the floor in the back of her car where nobody can see it. She doesn't have to act on it.

Madison leaves the house, setting the alarm and locking up behind herself. Their own house has an alarm system that Dad

38

disabled, because he and Mom and her brother and sister came and went so much, it made everybody crazy. Cheryl likes to set the alarm, not realizing it doesn't work. Nobody tells her, and she doesn't seem to notice that she's never billed for it. Maybe she thinks it comes with the house, like the garbage disposal in the sink.

Madison gets into her Celica. She loves to drive it, wash it, vacuum it and use the cup holders. It used to be her life's dream to have her own car. It took a few weeks for her to realize: it's only a car. The real dream, the one that won't come true, is to have a family, with a mother and father.

Madison backs out of the Emmers' driveway.

Like the Jeep, the Celica does not have automatic transmission. When Madison first got it, she had trouble finding reverse. But now she's got the gears down and she loves shifting. The engine's crescendo is so satisfying.

Madison takes the turnpike. She loves speed, too. If she gets there fast, she won't have time to think about this act of intentionally going home to see if she can stand it there and learn to love her family again. Her whole family. The dead ones and the guilty ones and even herself.

She's trembling, as if she's been living in Australia or China for decades and now, at last, home is in sight.

● ● ●

Jack prays to the God who has not yet answered his prayers. *This* time! Jack prays. You can't let me down *this* time, God. It's for Tris! You owe Tris one.

He has to have divine intervention. On his own, Jack has no power. Not in court, not with the media, not with the family lawyer, not with his sisters. "God!" he yells.

He reaches Route One. Nobody calls it that. It's called the Post Road. South of the Post Road, a narrow strip of land is packed tight with houses, and then come the beach and the Atlantic Ocean. North of the Post Road are railroad tracks and the turnpike. West stretches the rest of America.

Jack doesn't slow down at intersections, let alone stop. He feels as if he has insect eyes, with extra eyeballs on stalks. He can see through things and under things. Another mile and he shoots into the day-care parking lot. No BMW—Jack feels reasonably sure the TV guy will not travel in Aunt Cheryl's heavy gray Lincoln with the car seat in the back—but they could be here any second. Chances are, they already phoned.

He imagines Aunt Cheryl giving instructions to Tris's teacher, Brianna. "I want Tris to look really cute. If he's dirty, change him into his extra set of clothing. Brush his hair. Wash his face. He's going to be on TV! We're all going to be on TV! Yay!"

Jack takes a deep breath to subdue his heaving lungs. He doesn't want to look panicky. He often picks Tris up, so they're used to him here. But they'll know that on a Friday at noon, Jack should be in school.

The entrance is locked. No easy access to a day care. Jack presses the bell and the director says on the intercom, "Who is it?" which is annoying, because she can see him just fine; there's a camera. He smiles at the camera. "Jack Fountain. I'm here for Tris."

She buzzes him in.

Jack forces himself to stroll past the infant room, the art room and the kiddie computer room, all windowed into the hall, so every teacher can see everything. Teacher eyes follow Jack's progress.

In Tris's classroom a riot of balloons is painted over the walls and ceiling. The door is open, but a gate keeps the kids in. Tris is playing with a three-piece jigsaw puzzle. The best thing Tris has going for him is this place, where he's happy and busy, and they don't seem to care about an accident involving a little guy who didn't know what was happening. Tris's original day care refused to take him back, a decision that still twists Jack's gut.

Brianna is changing a little girl's diaper. Jack likes Brianna. He has never seen her treat Tris differently from the other kids. "Hi, Brianna."

She looks over her shoulder, surprised. "Jack! What's up? How come you're here?"

"Half day."

Brianna's only a few years out of high school. She knows the meaning of the lovely phrase "half day." She grins.

Jack steps over the gate and into the room. His little brother races over. "We had finger painting, Jack! Mine is blue! It isn't dry yet!"

"We'll leave it here till it dries," Jack says. "Because you and I are headed out." Jack is skin-crawly with nerves. Does he hear a car engine? Will the producer arrive, complete with cameras? Will Jack's attempt to snatch his brother from the jaws of reality TV end up on film?

He swings Tris up to sit on his hip. Tris isn't big. He's still easy to hold toddler style. "Have a nice weekend, Brianna. Say bye-bye, Tris." Jack steps back over the gate.

"Where are you going?" asks Brianna, not to rat on him, but so that next Monday, she can ask Tris about his big adventure.

Jack does not have the slightest idea where they are going. Plan A is to get Tris before Aunt Cheryl can. Plan B, and for that matter, Plans C through Z, haven't come to him yet. "Secret," whispers Jack loudly, so Tris is in on it.

Brianna is smiling. People love it that Jack stayed with Tris. It's weird to be popular just because he lives in his own house. Of course, his sisters partly bailed because of Aunt Cheryl, but the world doesn't know that. And they partly bailed because people made offers—you can stay with us; you can live here. Nobody made such an offer to Jack.

He gallops to the front door, but not fast enough. The day-care director is hurrying toward him. "Hey, Mrs. Griz," he says, aiming for casual. Her last name has more syllables, but nobody uses them.

Mrs. Griz bobs down the hall. "Your aunt just called!"

• • •

Smithy has no way to get home from this isolated boarding school. It's about an hour and a half to Boston, where she could get a train or a plane. There are no taxis in the nearby village, and hitchhiking is against the law. She doesn't have a car. No student has a car. No teacher will give her a ride. They'll give her counseling.

More counseling—can you imagine? "Have you come to terms with the accident?" they like to say.

Smithy no longer cares about the accident. She cares about going home.

She could ask Mrs. Murray to drive up and get her. But Diana's mother would probably say "Finish the semester, dear, and then come home."

Smith Fountain has finished the semester. She's finished mourning. She's finished being furious.

It's time.

She leaves the cafeteria and enters the big front hall, where her coat hangs on a hook, her book bag under it. Most of the school year in the hills of Massachusetts is during cold weather. Taking off and putting on coats, hats, scarves, mittens and boots are constants. Some kids deal by wearing nothing. They race from building to building in shirtsleeves, taunting the cold. Others wrap themselves like packages, blocking out every wisp of wind. This morning is very chilly, but nobody's in full winter gear yet. Smithy is wearing jeans, a long-sleeved white cotton shirt and a tangerine zip-up sweatjacket with a hood. She bought the jacket when she was staying with Kate and Kate's mother took them to the mall. Smithy loves using her own credit card. The card has a limit, but this person Wade just pays the bill, so it doesn't feel like a limit.

Idling on the pavement in front of her is a yellow school bus, like the one Smithy and Jack and Madison used to take back home. Smithy is calling it home again. Is it? Can she walk back in that door and be home? What will Jack and Madison say? Will they still like her?

Around her swarm kids who are in a great mood. It seems that two art classes are taking this bus to the Boston Museum of Fine Arts. There's nothing like a field trip to make kids laugh. Smithy bathes in their exuberance, as if she could rub it in like lotion.

The art teachers talk so intently to one another they could be plotting a murder. They climb onto the bus, leave their purses on the double front seat close to the driver and hop back out. One has a clipboard on which she checks off names.

There are not enough kids to fill the bus. Most kids prefer the back. Those seats fill immediately. Others scatter according to whatever friendships or lack of friendships they have in art class.

Smithy hangs her book bag back up. She fishes out her little purse, slides her cell phone into her jeans pocket and pulls the hood of her sweatshirt over her head. Not that tangerine is camouflage.

One teacher returns to the building for a last stop in the ladies' room. The other teacher and the driver stand on the sidewalk, studying a map.

Smithy boards the bus.

◆　◆　◆

Madison turns left on Chesmore Road.

Connecticut is tree-covered. There are no long views. Even

in fall, when the bare branches of maples are like ink drawings against the sky, the thick green hemlocks and pines keep each house a secret from the next.

She can't see her house yet. She isn't ready to see it, either. Her gut clutches.

She stops several houses short of her own. She hasn't mastered parallel parking. But she likes pulling over as if she *could* parallel park. Madison gets close to the curb and turns off the engine.

Cheryl is probably at home. What is Madison going to say about being gone all this time and now being back?

It's my house. I don't need to give an explanation.

Her mouth is dry.

She thinks of Tris. Against all odds, Madison loves the tiny brother who entered their lives at such high cost. She was the best at getting baby Tris to fall asleep. She rocked, sang, swaddled and walked the floor. Tris was always exactly the right weight in her arms. She loved his scent after a bath, the amazed expression on his little face when he started noticing the world, the belly laugh when Madison nibbled his bare toes.

I've missed Daddy's birthday. But I haven't missed Tris's. I'm home in time for his third birthday.

She locks the Celica, even though this may be the lowest-crime zip code in the nation, and walks toward her house. The jutting garage will prevent Cheryl from seeing Madison approach. First, she'll peek in the garage window to see if Cheryl's big Lincoln is sitting there. Then she'll decide.

A van passes Madison. It's white. Medium-sized. No windows

45

except for the front seats. It sports a television station logo. On the roof is a tower of antennae, to let you know this isn't a repair vehicle. It's the camera crew.

Madison never knew how the camera crews of last year arrived in the driveway so fast. Who called them? How had they known that Dad's death was a story they'd want to follow for days? The TV van parked on Chesmore Road had induced strangers to stop and neighbors to call. Everybody wanted to be in on it. Television sucked them forward, like incredibly strong lips sucking on a straw, slurping every drop of the Fountain children's lives.

Madison slows her pace, waiting for the TV van to leave Chesmore.

But it does not leave. It turns into a driveway.

Madison's heart falls while her body rockets forward. No! It can't be *her* driveway!

But it is.

Something is wrong. What's left to go wrong? Anything that can go wrong already has!

Oh, Tris! Oh, Jack! Please be all right! I'm not back yet!

Madison races to her front door.

Four

THE BUS IS HALFWAY TO BOSTON. NOBODY HAS ASKED SMITHY why she's on the trip, probably because there are two classes and everybody figures she's in the other one. She's sitting alone, and maybe they figure she wants to be alone, although who ever does? But they're not interfering.

Smithy is lying down, curled up on the two-person bench so the teachers won't turn around and spot her. Her skull is pressed against the armrest and her feet are twisted as if somebody is trying to pull them off.

I left my postcards in my room, she thinks.

Nothing else, not a single possession or piece of clothing, matters to her now. How strange. Because Smithy resented the postcards when they came.

Every week Nonny sent a postcard to each grandchild. Over the years, she'd sent hundreds of them. Nonny wrote exactly the same message to every grandchild every time. *Love you. Love, Nonny.* When Nonny and Poppy visited the boarding school,

Nonny bought a stack of postcards, and Smithy got card after card featuring her own location.

Love you. Love, Nonny.

Nonny and Poppy live far away. They are mainly loved because Mom and Dad said to love them. In fact, they are strangers who work hard in ordinary jobs, fifty weeks a year, and cannot easily visit. The few times they were able to come east, Dad bought their plane tickets. Nonny is a waitress. Poppy works in an office supply store. They enjoy their work. Their activities—gardening, church choir, softball league, line dancing, driving for Meals On Wheels—do not interest Smithy.

Mainly the children know their grandparents by video connection. Once a week, at a prearranged time, Mom and Dad used to prime the children with topics to discuss: a school project, a ballet step, a sleepover. When they no longer had parents to set this up, it didn't happen. Smithy and Madison couldn't stand sitting in front of that screen, pretending to be happy, chatting with grandparents who were also pretending to be happy.

Last summer, Nonny and Poppy took all their precious vacation time and traveled out east. They tried to collect the children for a reunion. Smithy was in summer school, but they drove up to see her. She lied and maneuvered to spend as little time with them as possible. Her grandparents, who love her.

And yet it is with Nonny that Smithy has had the most profound conversation of her life.

Tris wasn't born yet. Smithy was eleven. She and Nonny were sitting on the tired old sofa pushed against the wall in the big kitchen/family room, tucked under one of Mom's knit blankets.

Mom liked color. No soft denim blue or vanilla lace. It was a wallop-you-in-the-eyes combination of orange and red.

(Where is that blanket now? Where is anything now? The old saggy couch was the first thing Cheryl got rid of, when she was in charge at last.)

On that day, Nonny and Smithy were alone. Mom was napping, Dad at work, Madison at a friend's house, Jack at a ball game.

Outside, the picketers chanted. The picketers weren't early risers, which meant that Smithy and Jack and Madison could get to school without running into them. It was coming home that was tricky. Dad rented Nonny and Poppy a car with tinted windows so nobody could see in, and they picked the kids up at school, drove into the garage and waited for the automatic door to close behind them before anybody got out.

"Do you think Mom is doing the right thing?" Smithy dared to ask her grandmother.

"I don't know if it's right. But it is extraordinary. Your mother is brave. Any mother would lay down her life for her baby *after* it's born. But your mother is laying down her life for her baby *before* it's born."

A fifty percent chance, the doctor said, when he told Mom about her cancer. But only if she started chemo immediately.

"I'm going to have a baby, though," said their mother. "Chemo would damage my baby."

The doctor wasn't interested. "Get rid of it," he said, shrugging.

At dinner, Mom repeated this conversation to her husband

and her three children, who thought they would talk about dessert or the possibility of quitting piano lessons. "What do you get rid of?" demanded Laura Fountain. "Broken toys. Stained shirts. Not your baby."

Smithy was not paying attention to the baby part. She was paying attention to the cancer part. Her mother had a fifty percent chance of dying?

"This baby," announced their mother, and she was smiling—Smithy always remembers that smile—"is your brother or sister. I want him. Or her. Because our fourth baby will be wonderful, just like you."

A few days later, an ultrasound established that it was a boy. Mom was beaming. "He's healthy," she said excitedly.

"You're not," pointed out the doctor. "You have to start chemo."

"No. I can make it," said Mom confidently. "I'm tough. It's only five more months. I'll start chemo after the baby's here."

"You'll be dead before then. This cancer is invasive. You have to have chemo. We don't have other weapons," said the doctor brutally.

Mom shrugged. She'd be the weapon. Her own determination would save her. She carefully prepared her children for what the doctors insisted would happen, but she always added a disclaimer: "I'll whip it." Did she believe this? Or was it a gift to her children? Smithy never knew, because the end came so swiftly, there was no time for questions or answers.

But on that day, on that sofa, Smithy buried her face against her grandmother, and Nonny said, "When I was a girl, decades ago, we said the baby always comes first. Now people say the mother always comes first. We say women have the right to make a choice, but we don't mean it. We believe they have to make a particular choice. Here we are in your own house with the curtains pulled and the shades down so that strangers who accuse your mother of suicide and want to force her to have chemo can't see in. Your mother isn't paying attention. She's made her choice and she's ready."

"I'm not ready," whispered Smithy.

"Neither am I. But you know what, Smithy? You and your brother and sister have strong names. Smith. Jack. Madison. Those aren't wimpy, weak, washout names. Those are names for people who lift their chins and keep going and wake up smiling. That's what your mother is counting on. And so am I."

Lying on the bench in the school bus in the fetal position, Smithy admits at last why she doesn't answer her grandparents' e-mails, or send postcards of her own, or hang out with them when they visit.

Smithy didn't lift her chin and keep going. She cannot be counted on.

The bus hits a bump and flings Smithy half off the seat. She struggles to a sitting position, rubbing her eyes to make it look as if she'd been sleeping, rather than weeping.

They have not hit a bump. They are here. The teachers are already off the bus. Kids gather their stuff and exit single file.

Smithy isn't ready. She needs more time before she makes her decision. After all, she loves boarding school. It tells you what to do. It's the most organized, well-packed box of life out there. If Smithy runs from boarding school, she's smashing this life, too.

Smithy steps into the aisle. Walks forward. Now she's next to the driver. She's on the top step.

The teachers move toward the museum entrance.

Smithy tugs her tangerine hood over her hair, steps off the bus, goes the other way around it and crosses the street in the middle of the block. When she gauges that the bulk of the bus is between her and the museum entrance, she glances back.

Nobody is looking.

She flies down the sidewalk, galloping to the corner. Safely around the bend, she flags a taxi. "Back Bay Station, please." Smithy sinks down in the seat as if enemy agents are after her.

She has no idea what the train schedule is, but she's in luck. There's a train at eleven-forty. She buys the ticket with her rarely used ATM card and decides to get a hundred dollars cash back. The twenty-dollar bills are so exciting to a person who leads a shopping-free life. She has a vision of hitting the malls with her sister, and Madison saying, Why would I want your company? You didn't want ours.

Smithy gets a blueberry muffin, an orange juice and a fashion magazine and finds a seat. She can't eat, drink or turn the pages. The art teachers may not realize they are down one student, but some kid will say, "Where's Smithy?" and panic will set in. The field trip will be ruined and the teachers will be in trouble.

Smithy needs to notify the school. She'll wait until the train leaves the station and they can't get her back. Then she'll text, that wonderful method of communication where you aren't available for questioning.

They can't arrest me for going home, she tells herself. Aunt Cheryl can't ship me back, either. I'm too old and tall for shipping.

Suddenly she is wildly happy.

* * *

Mrs. Griz pats her hair and straightens her blouse. "Your aunt Cheryl is on her way over here with a friend of hers," she tells Jack. "A producer! He's looking into doing a television special."

How well Jack remembers this tone of voice. The hot, thick anticipation of somebody who might get on TV.

After they gave him Dad's wallet and watch, a friendly cop drove him home from the hospital. His sisters were told by phone that Dad hadn't made it. (That was what the adults said: "Your father didn't make it." As if it were Dad's fault.)

Somehow Jack got out of that police car. The door felt exceptionally heavy. His body seemed equally heavy, and hard to maneuver.

In spite of the cold, everybody was still outside.

Madison and Smithy were near the Jeep, staring at nothing. They looked very thin and young. They were not wearing jackets. They were shivering.

Aunt Cheryl was out on the faded grass, reciting her story to a garden of microphones, which stuck up like metal flowers in her face. Tris, no longer crying, sat on the bottom step of the front porch, absorbed by a favorite toy—a heavy-duty picture book with magnetized cardboard cars to drive around the illustrations. He had a cylinder of Oreo cookies that one of his sisters must have brought to keep him quiet.

Tris was weirdly alone: no aunt and no sister near him. Only television cameras. When Tris saw Jack, he broke into his beautiful smile and offered his brother a cookie. Unusually for a two-year-old, Tris loved to share. Jack made it over to his baby brother and lifted him up—Oreos, picture book, magnets and all.

Into Jack's face was thrust a microphone held by a pretty blond woman Jack recognized from the local news. She was always pacing down the main street of some area town, asking how people felt about the weather or the price of gasoline. She leaned toward Jack. "How do you feel?" she said lovingly.

Jack's eyes didn't focus. That was how he felt.

He took a step toward his house, and she took one too, moving the microphone even closer. "Your baby brother killed your mother by being born. Now the same little brother has killed your father. How do you feel toward him?"

Jack dropped the toys, but not his brother, planning to smash the woman's mouth and the terrible question she'd shoved at him. The officer blocked him, fast enough to stop Jack's fist from connecting but not fast enough to camouflage the attempt. This moment was one of the most-watched videos on the Internet that week.

Now, at the exit to her day-care center, Mrs. Griz stands as close to Jack as that microphone was. "It's so exciting," she whispers. "TV crews right here!"

Tris loves words. He repeats anything Jack says, so if Jack is studying chemistry, and Tris sits with him, the next day he'll hear Tris murmur, "Covalent. pH scale." Jack cannot repeat anything Mrs. Griz says or Tris will pick it up. "Pretty neat, huh?" says Jack. "Be sure to get all the details ironed out," he adds, going out the door. "I have a half day in school, so Tris and I are headed for a soccer game. Have a nice weekend."

Outside, Jack lowers Tris into the child seat on the back of his bike. It takes forever to strap Tris in and get his helmet fastened, because Jack's fingers have thickened and he fumbles. Tris wants to know what's in Jack's backpack, but Jack doesn't feel like discussing it. Tris moves on to the secret adventure. "Smithy plays soccer. Are we going to see Smithy?"

When it all went down, Smithy enrolled herself in boarding school. Fourteen years old and she figured out how. Jack is still amazed. He never figured out anything. After the funeral, after Nonny and Poppy flew back to Missouri, Jack was possessed by the fear that he would somehow lose another member of his family. He didn't go out for sports. When each school day was over, he rushed home to do a head count.

He was right to be afraid. In a matter of weeks, both his sisters left.

Tris mainly knows Smithy from the scrapbook. Jack can see Mom now, sitting up in bed, choosing photographs, writing captions, ensuring that her fourth baby would have something to remember her by. Tris sleeps with it, as if it's a bunny or a blankie. The most-requested bedtime story is for Jack to go through the album. "And this is Daddy," Jack will say, pointing. "And this is

Mommy. Here's Madison playing tennis. Here's Smithy playing soccer. And here is baby Tris."

"We aren't going to see Smithy today," he tells Tris. Or ever, as far as Jack knows. Sometimes he misses his sisters so much he goes into his failure-to-breathe mode. Other times he can't even remember what they look like.

Jack has no choice of roads. He has to leave the day care by the same route he came in. He checks traffic. No BMW. No Lincoln. He crosses the Post Road, turns down a side street that won't take Cheryl to the day care, so it's probably safe, and now he is approaching the railroad station.

They are on the Boston to New York track, but no through trains stop here. This is a local commuter station. The city of New Haven is its only destination; people continuing to New York have to change trains. But even if Jack and Tris could hop on a train and get out of here, then what? You have to have supper wherever you're going. You have to sleep somewhere. Take a shower in the morning. Have breakfast. Jack literally doesn't have a dime, but even if he had a thousand dollars, how could he run with a three-year-old?

Jack's only reliable rescuer is Diana. But this isn't babysitting for an hour. This is Tris's life—weeks and months and years in which Jack has to protect his little brother, because that's what he promised.

"You be the best big brother there is, okay?" said his mother. She was too weak to sit up, but she was smiling because the baby was healthy. "He's going to have a good life," she told Jack. "Now you help Daddy. He's going to need you and this is hard for him."

"I'll help Daddy," he promised. He was twelve. He didn't know how bad it was going to get. But neither did Mom.

How is Jack to give Tris this good life Mom had in mind? Being featured as a monster and a parent killer on national TV is not going to launch Tris on a good life. One good thing, Jack realizes: Cheryl won't stick Tris in foster care when she's portraying herself as the Good Aunt, the Only Hope, the woman these children are So Lucky to have.

And now Jack has to call the girls, which he hates doing. He gets caught somewhere between desperation and anger, between love and hate, and can think of nothing acceptable to say. But he has to tell them about the docudrama plan and make sure they don't cooperate. Smithy can hide out pretty well up there in Massachusetts. But Madison . . . Is Cheryl telling the truth? Are the Emmers trying to get rid of her? Jack wants her home on any terms. Yet if Madison is forced to come home, what will that be like?

Jack reconsiders flight.

If he takes off with Tris, Aunt Cheryl will call the police. She'll love calling the police. Any attention is good attention. Jack running away would just add more scope. And bringing in the police could help Cheryl. Aside from creating a nice scene in a docudrama, if Jack runs away from home with a three-year-old and no money in cold weather on a bike, Cheryl can probably put *Jack* in foster care.

So there's nowhere to run.

But if he takes Tris home, they walk into the arms of the producer.

Tris is chattering about nothing, strings of marvelous words and miscellaneous thoughts. He reaches up under Jack's jacket and latches his fingers on to the belt loops of Jack's jeans.

Jack's emotions suck the strength out of him. He's barely pedaling. The bike is coming to a stop.

* * *

The rear of the TV van in Madison's driveway opens up and people climb out, as if they're appliance deliverymen. Madison is running as fast as she can. She circles the van and almost smashes into a little blue car. Leaping up the steps, she rips open the front door, and plows to a halt.

Cheryl is standing right there, badly startled by Madison's sudden entrance, which is reasonable, because Madison hasn't walked through this door since Labor Day.

Beside her is a middle-aged man.

Cheryl is well dressed, as if she's off to a bridge game and luncheon at a fine restaurant. She's a heavy woman who carries her weight well. Her hair is dyed ash-blond and around her throat a scarf is pinned at a jaunty angle. She's just had a manicure in her favorite dark vermilion polish, a sort of dead red. Cheryl's fingers are long and attractive and she's proud of them. She does not seem frightened or worried, so maybe nothing's happening. But then what's up with the television van?

Cheryl's amazement gives way to a smug little smile. "Madison. Darling. What a treat." She rests her fingers lightly on Madison's shoulders and gives her air kisses.

Madison is not a treat. Madison has consistently been the rude kid in the family, the one who never calls this woman Aunt, because she isn't one.

Mom's mother, Grandma Smith, died when Madison was little. Poor Grandpa Smith, in a moment of loneliness, remarried a woman with an adult daughter named Cheryl. The second marriage was not just a mistake—it was a disaster. It was over almost before it began. There was an embarrassing divorce. When Grandpa had a heart attack a few years later, neither the ex-wife nor the ex-stepdaughter came to his funeral, which was fine, because hardly anybody remembered that they existed.

Mom had been dead more than a year when Cheryl Rand appeared at their door. Such a tragedy! she cried. I just heard! I'm going through a career change, taking time off to find myself. Please let me pitch in and help my dear dead sister's family.

In what way, Madison wanted to know, were Laura Fountain and Cheryl Rand dear to each other? Laura Fountain—sender of Christmas, Easter, Thanksgiving, Halloween and Valentine's Day cards—did not have Cheryl in her address book. Laura Fountain—happy keeper of a thick birthday diary—did not have Cheryl's birthday listed either.

Dad let Cheryl have the guest room for a day or two because he couldn't think of a nice way to say no. Cheryl was a huge help. From groceries on the shelf to laundry in the drawers, from driving the older children to their circuit of games and rehearsals and orthodontic appointments and friends' houses, to returning videos on time and being home for the furnace repairman, Cheryl smoothed out their chaotic household.

Cheryl loved the house itself, not the family. She did not take care of Tris, who continued to attend day care, dropped off and picked up by Dad. Dad frequently muttered something about "sending Cheryl packing," but instead he paid her a salary. He tried to treat her like an employee and not a pretend aunt, but Cheryl wasn't having it. If Dad introduced her as Ms. Rand, she'd say, "I'm the children's aunt Cheryl."

What has it been like for Jack living with this woman all these months?

Madison's gut shudders at the extent to which she has abandoned her brothers.

Next to Cheryl, in Madison's front hall, stands a middle-aged man Madison has never seen before. A smile inches across his face and gets a good grip. He extends his hand for Madison to shake. Bringing his other hand forward, he clasps hers in both of his.

He's staring at her way too intently. What has she stepped into? Is Cheryl dating this man? When he abandons her hand, Madison feels in her pocket, checking for her cell phone, in case she needs to call 911.

"Madison, a joy to meet you. I'm Angus Nicolson. I'm a television producer. You've come at just the right time. Your aunt and I have wonderful news. You're going to be on television!" he proclaims, clearly expecting Madison to jump up and down with joy. "We're setting up a beautiful, gentle program, in which we'll follow the tragic circumstances of your beautiful family. Your case is so unusual, so heartrending."

Madison has picked the absolute worst minute to come home. A media minute.

This man is standing here as if he owns the place, because he thinks he does. That's what it is to be television.

The Fountains have faced the media three times: Mom's decision, then Mom's death, then Dad's death. To the media, this is not a grieving family. It's a story. It's public property. More precisely, it's their property.

"Let's all sit down for a little chat," says Angus Nicolson, his arm encircling her. "Madison, you are just a beautiful young woman. I can't wait to do a screen test on you."

Cheryl can barely restrain herself. She presses her fingertips together, jouncing them, a sort of clapping prayer position.

Behind Angus Nicolson stands a short, squat woman with no makeup, her hair falling out of a casual ponytail, her sweatshirt baggy and her jeans old. She has a notebook in her hand and a camera on a strap. It isn't an impressive movie camera—not the big, sturdy kind that takes a strong shoulder. But it will film.

The children had to wade through the media to attend their own mother's funeral. As for Dad's, when it became clear that gawkers, reporters and distant acquaintances would fill the pews, the minister suggested a private funeral; the following day, he'd hold a memorial service open to the public, which the children need not attend.

Cheryl had been opposed to anything private. People kept asking her what she'd seen of the accident, and she kept telling them. She loved telling them. She wept well in public.

The children were unable to argue and the minister lost the argument with Cheryl.

Don't look at the cameras, Reverend Phillips advised the children. And don't use the reporters' names. A name lets them creep into your life.

Angus Nicolson and the woman with bad hair are not creeping. They are staking a claim, and Cheryl is glad.

Five

SMITHY HAS A FEELING THE HEADMISTRESS WON'T LIKE SLANG OR abbreviations. Carefully she texts:

> Dear Dr. Dresser, Sorry to worry you. Going home for good by train. Thanks for everything. Smith Fountain.

There. The boarding-school stage of Smithy's life is over.

She stares out the window as the New York–bound train whips past little Massachusetts stations. Normal towns, where normal commuters park in normal lots, have normal jobs and go home to normal families.

When it happened—when Smithy's family was forever separated from "normal"—Smithy was in her bedroom. She wasn't paying attention to anything or anybody. She was online, happily seeing what various friends had posted. The scream alerted her. Who had screamed—Cheryl in horror, Dad in agony, a neighbor in shock?

The scream pitched Smithy out of her chair and out of her

house. There at the edge of the driveway stood Aunt Cheryl. Her hands were over her mouth and strange bleating sounds were coming out. The Jeep was halfway down the driveway. Madison was bending over something.

Their father.

When the long day had finally ended, something was wrong in Smithy's brain. She could no longer see in color. Television was blurry, leaping nonsense, so she stopped watching. She couldn't hear well either. Music was racket. She stopped listening. She seemed to swim in slow motion through a black-and-white movie filled with strangers.

Nonny and Poppy flew in. Smithy had trouble recognizing them. They were desperately sad: they had outlived their only child. They stood, or swayed, or sat with no more idea what to do next than the children.

In the street, strangers gathered. Cars slowed down. Reporters flocked. A tabloid newspaper fell in love with the tragedy. "Baby Boy Kills Dad" was one day's headline. "Toddler Who Caused Mother's Death Now Causes Father's" was another.

"What can we do to help?" their grandparents asked Cheryl.

"Everything's under control. You just sit on the sofa," said Cheryl, scurrying to give another interview.

Nonny took Tris into the spacious kitchen, where the old couch was tight against the wall. Tris rode his toddler trike over the vinyl floor, around the kitchen island and up to the sofa, where he chatted with anybody sitting there.

One day a reporter took photographs right through the kitchen window. Nonny called the police. Then she pulled the little curtains so nobody could see in. Nobody could see out, either. The room, like their hearts, was dark.

Nobody knew what to do with Tris. He just went on being Tris. He was two. He didn't know anything. Every now and then he asked for Daddy. "Daddy come home now?"

Because he was cute and smart and always surrounded by an adoring family, Tris expected everybody to look at him. He had no idea that they were looking at him differently.

Now they will look at Smithy differently. She bailed on her own family. Okay, fine, she's home again. But is she marked, just as Tris is marked?

. . .

Angus Nicolson continues to beam at Madison. "We were on our way to the day care to get little Tristan, but we can do that later. Let's sit down together, in your beautiful living room, with all the lovely colors your aunt chose. Gosh, what a warm and homey place this is. Of course I know you miss your poor mother so much. Come tell me about it."

A cameraman opens the door without knocking and shoulders his way in.

"And of course, we're counting on you, the big sister," says Angus, "to lead the way."

Madison hears her mother: "You can handle this, darling. I'm counting on you. You're the big sister."

This is what has killed Madison all these months. She may be the big sister, but she's not the one anybody counts on.

"It's the anniversary, you see," Angus says, as if Madison could have forgotten any of those terrible dates. She wants to scream, "You go near my little brother and I will rip your pathetic little smile right off your pathetic little plastic-surgeried face!" She remembers in time that there are cameras here. Great footage—the sister who runs out on her family spitting about the baby brother, as if she actually loves Tris and has a right to opinions.

I do love Tris, thinks Madison.

This is huge.

The knowledge envelops the hallway and the people standing there. It inflates Madison's lungs and softens her heart. *She does love Tris.*

It's why she's home. She needs to tell her brothers she's sorry, that she loves them. Will they give her another chance? She needs Mom and Dad to be listening—and maybe they are, because Madison cannot believe that they're just so much roadkill; they have to *be* somewhere, waiting for Madison to come home.

First, the home needs to be emptied of strangers. "Cheryl, did you invite these people here?"

"Madison, you are not part of this household anymore. I make the decisions."

"What decision did you make?"

"I feel it can only help us, Maddy, in our divided situation, to air things in front of a psychiatrist and begin to feel our way forward into healing."

"In other words, you called a TV station and asked them to do some sort of program."

"Not some sort of program," says Angus Nicolson warmly. He is still smiling. The smile is a separate creature that lives on his face and has nothing to do with his words. "An in-depth look, Madison. It will be cleansing. It will bring out the facts. It will showcase you and your sister and brother as the beautiful people you are, and your aunt as the fine woman you are so fortunate to have."

Madison must not do anything that could merit recording such as bare her teeth and snarl. She walks into the kitchen as if there's nothing on her mind but a good snack. She stops dead.

There is not one trace of Laura Fountain left in her own kitchen. Mom's sunny yellow paint is now beige. Her shelves of cookbooks have been replaced by rows of collectible snow babies. The tiny oil paintings of red-hot zinnias are gone. The front of the refrigerator displays no children's art. The wooden platter of lemons and limes is not there. Even the dish towels are not Mom's.

Angus is breathing on her hair, a creepy little breeze. "You and I, Madison, we'll start getting acquainted today. Lay the groundwork."

Madison wants to kick holes in walls and dents in shins. Instead, she detours around Angus and takes the stairs. "I don't have time for chitchat. I'm just here to pick up a few things in my room."

She doesn't think even a television producer will have the nerve to follow her, but she's wrong. Angus trots right up. "I'm going to the bathroom," says Madison. She stands motionless, midstairs, until he yields and goes back down.

Madison slides gratefully into the sanctuary of her room. The quilt Mom made out of Madison's summer camp T-shirts is not in evidence. Not one poster, book jacket or CD cover is still taped to the wall.

In the middle of a bare desk—in her whole life, Madison has never had a bare desk—lies a stack of postcards. She doesn't have to read them. *Love you. Love, Nonny,* they say. Madison's eyes prickle. Her grandmother has kept writing, every week, putting that stamp on, going to the post office, the way she has since the day Madison learned to read. It doesn't seem like Cheryl to save the postcards. It must be Jack.

Madison doesn't communicate with anybody if she can avoid it. And still the postcards come. *Love you. Love, Nonny.*

Madison wants her parents so fiercely she's afraid she'll bawl. The sound of sobs will bring the TV crew running. She feels her way down the hall to her parents' room as if she's gone blind.

The worst has happened. Cheryl Rand's jewelry is strewn on Mom's dresser. Cheryl Rand's makeup collection covers both Mom's and Dad's side of the bathroom counter. This is no longer the house of Reed and Laura Fountain.

Then it hits her.

These people—this Angus, this bad hair woman, that camera crew—are on their way to get Tris at the day care. They don't mean to pick him up. They mean to get him on film.

◆ ◆ ◆

Dr. Dresser summons Kate to the administration building.

Kate is terrified. Either somebody she loves has been in a car accident or she's failed some crucial test of knowledge or moral character. But when she bursts into Dr. Dresser's office, the woman simply looks annoyed. "It seems that Smith Fountain stowed away

68

on the art class bus trip to Boston. Did she discuss her plans with you?"

Kate is astonished. Why on earth would anybody stow away on a bus trip to the Museum of Fine Arts? Especially Smithy?

"Smith texted me," says Dr. Dresser. "She claims to be on the train, going home. I called her aunt. Mrs. Rand is thrilled. Clapping, in fact. She says the timing is just right. What timing, Kate? What is going on? Is Smithy really on the train?"

Smithy finds time to text Dr. Dresser but not Kate? On a train, where there's nothing but time? Her own roommate! Her best friend on campus! The one Kate's never interrogated in spite of the thousand questions she has. This roommate runs away and Kate is the last to know? "She didn't say anything," says Kate casually.

Dr. Dresser glares at her, clearly believing Kate knows every detail. After some pointless arguing, Dr. Dresser lets her go.

Kate leaves the administration building. The empty campus looks alien. She is not in the mood for class. She storms back to their room. *Her* room, now that Smithy's abandoned it.

When four hundred kids find out that Smith Fountain hasn't even bothered to let her roommate know she's running away from boarding school—a thing Kate has never even heard of, because if you want to leave, you just call your family and they come!—Kate will have to lie and tell everybody she knew all along.

She's too angry to cry. After all she's done for Smithy!

When Smithy arrived last February, the only new kid for second semester, Dr. Dresser gave Kate a brief outline of Smithy's situation and told her to be understanding. Kate mostly understood that she wanted to get on the Internet and do a little research. The results of that research were so shocking, Kate figured this girl Smithy would cry herself to sleep every night.

But Smithy, thanks to Kate, adjusted perfectly. They are good roommates and best friends, and Smithy is a welcome houseguest over many long weekends and every vacation.

Kate finds a pack of cheese-and-peanut-butter crackers, flings herself backward on her mattress and rips open the cellophane. Too bad she can't rip Smithy as easily.

What a traitor.

• • •

A phone is ringing. Madison pays no attention. For months, she has lived where any phone call is for the Emmers, and any call for Madison is to her cell. She can hear Cheryl answering downstairs in the front hall, where there's a fat old telephone on a small table below a large mirror. Mom used to love that phone; she said it made her feel like an actress in a 1960s movie.

Madison shuts the door to Mom and Dad's bedroom so she can think. She is the oldest. She has to behave like it for a change.

Step one. Don't let these people near Tris.

At Dad's desk, now Cheryl's, Madison flips through the phone book, finds the number for Tris's day care, and calls on her cell phone. Madison tries to remember the woman's real name. She does not want to use that silly nickname, Griz.

"Cradle Care," a voice answers.

It comes to her. "May I please speak to Mrs. Grisjevsky?"

Madison moves Cheryl's mouse pad. Underneath are the carved initials RF. Madison traces them with her finger.

"This is Mrs. Griz."

Deep breath. "This is Madison Fountain, Tris Fountain's sister. I understand from Mrs. Rand, my mother's former stepsister, that there is a plan to film my brother during the hours he is entrusted to your care. You know that it would not be good for a little boy to suffer even more, and I know you'd never agree to allow your wonderful school to be invaded by people who don't care what happens to Tris. So I'm calling to reinforce your decision not to allow it. Mrs. Rand has her heart set on a TV documentary. But I know you'll put Tris first, as you always have, thinking only of what's best for him." Madison's hands are sweaty.

"But they're on their way," says Mrs. Griz wistfully.

Television. It's like some sort of god. People yearn to bow in front of it, to please it, to be part of it. Madison tries again. "They can't get inside unless you buzz them in."

Mrs. Griz says nothing.

Madison has no more arguments, so she closes the conversation briskly and cheerfully. "Thanks, Mrs. Griz. I knew Tris could depend on you." Tris knew he could depend on his big sister Madison, too, and look where it got him.

Mrs. Griz speaks quickly. "Since Jack picked Tris up early, of course they won't be recording today. We'll just discuss *details* today. I'm *sure* there's a way to please *every*body." In other words, she's totally on board with the TV plan.

Madison disconnects without saying good-bye. Nice mature behavior, she compliments herself sarcastically.

71

Jack has already picked Tris up? That sounds like him, sacrificing all for his little brother. But Friday during school? Do they have a half day or something?

He'll tell her when they talk. Luckily these people don't know about her car—well, Cheryl knows, but Cheryl is way too excited to ask herself how Madison got here.

Madison cannot summon the courage to phone Jack, who once again is doing the right thing—saving Tris—as opposed to Madison, who drove up by accident, stumbled into a situation and can't even call off the day-care part. Madison takes the coward's way out and texts Jack.

* * *

The headmistress studies her paper folder on Elizabeth Smith Fountain. Smithy is a great kid, but then, Dr. Dresser thinks most of her students are great kids. What Smithy mainly is, is stranded. And like a beached sea creature, she's hard to help.

Dr. Dresser thinks of the stepaunt who has never, not once, driven up to visit. The stepaunt who was laughing, maybe even snickering, at the idea of Smithy heading home.

Dr. Dresser picks up the phone.

* * *

Jack has to buy himself some time.

Normally Cheryl couldn't care less when Jack takes Tris. But this is different: it interferes with Cheryl's plans to get on television. She is never without her cell phone, so he texts.

Tris + I at soccer game. Home 4 supper.

This too presents problems. It's now twelve-fifteen. What's he going to do for the next five or six hours? No three-year-old boy—and for that matter, no fifteen-year-old boy—can just sit around that long.

Jack can't believe he's still fifteen. He feels as if he's been fifteen for years. The Fountain family dates pile up in winter—Dad and Tris with November birthdays, Jack and Madison in January, Smithy in February. Oh, to be sixteen.

Even the slowest pedaling eventually moves a bike to the next block. Jack is now approaching the library. The pretty little central dome is what's left of the original library from 1888. Wings have been added every twenty or thirty years. The children's room, extending out the back, is the newest.

Jack locks his bike to the rack, in full view of every arriving vehicle. Not that Cheryl reads, uses the library or would think of coming here. Still.

"Where's the soccer game?" asks Tris.

"It starts later," says Jack, which isn't wholly a lie. If there were a soccer game and they were going, it would start later.

Tris is fine with that because he loves the library. Freed from his bicycle seat, he races on ahead. "I'm going to climb the tree!" he shouts, because the children's room features a tree house to read in. "And drive the boat!" because there's a real dinghy filled with pillows. "And then build castles!" because the fat red cardboard bricks are such fun to pile up and knock down.

The picture-book side of the children's wing is filled with bins, low tilted shelves and regular library shelves. Jack takes an armchair, but this isn't good enough for Tris, who races from one tree house window to the next. "Watch me, Jack!" he shouts. Jack circles below him, saying, "I see you!"

Jack often wonders what Tris thinks about. Tris lives in the present, as far as Jack can tell. At least, he hopes so, because the past is grim and the future is iffy.

His cell phone rings. Dreading Cheryl's response, Jack looks at his phone through slitted eyelids.

It's Madison. He's astonished. Madison, calling Friday during school? Madison, calling ever?

"No cell phones!" calls the distant librarian in a friendly voice. Jack nods and waves. He reads the text.

> am home. cheryl plans tv show 4 tris. Where r u?
> must talk.

Jack is sick. Cheryl already has Madison lined up. Madison's job is to bring Jack around.

He's been thinking of his sisters as allies. Unavailable, but allies. Of course this isn't true. They are so completely not allies that they don't even stay home and pretend.

At first, when Madison's godparents took her for the weekend, Jack figured she'd be home on Monday. But she was gone all the next week, as if there were no such thing as school. Then he found out Madison had enrolled in another school! The Emmers' school district! She came home for clothes and Jack tried to ask her about it, but he couldn't form a sentence.

His younger sister had no convenient godparents. Mom and Dad didn't get around to booking people for that duty with Smithy or Jack. What Smithy had was a set of beloved mystery books where the heroine lives at boarding school. Smithy went online, did a little research, presented a convincing argument to their trustee, Wade, and in a few weeks, she too left home.

Where r u? must talk.

Madison is right about that. Jack has to make her see how lousy this is. He can't call from here, not with the librarian eyeing him. He can't have Tris listening, either. And now that Tris is happy up in the tree house, he won't want to leave. Jack will have to drag him out, and Tris will grab table legs and computer wires to prevent it from happening. Jack doesn't have the time or energy for a scene. "Do you have to go potty?" he whispers up to Tris. "Want to go out in the woods with me and spray a tree? Like beagles?"

Tris is thrilled. He opens his mouth to shout "Yes!" but Jack puts up a finger. "Ssshhh. It's a secret. Librarians don't like it. We have to tiptoe."

Tris lets Jack swing him down from the tree house and to-gether they sneak out of the library to return Madison's message and piss on a few trees. Jack can think of a few people he'd like to piss on.

• • •

Smithy stares out the window. The route is low on scenery—the backs of warehouses and a gravel pit. But the road home is al-ways beautiful. Even when you're scared of home.

Smithy holds her cell phone like a pet, stroking it, soothed by it. Maybe she'll text her brother and sister. During the next pass-ing period between classes, they'll check for messages. Then they'll know she's on her way. They'll have time to think about it, get ready for it. And maybe be glad about it.

The train crosses Rhode Island. In a minute, Smithy will be in Connecticut.

The train does not stop at her own town. She can get off in Saybrook, which comes first, or ride past her town and get off in New Haven. Either way means a fifteen- or twenty-minute drive to her house. She'll need a ride. She has to call Cheryl.

The train is now in Connecticut. Smithy is breathing hard, as if approaching a finish line where there will be a ribbon to break.

We can be a normal family, she tells herself. Well, okay, we can be a family.

She's smiling when the phone rings.

It's Cheryl.

76

Six

MADISON STEELS HERSELF TO WADE THROUGH THE CROWD OF staring strangers at the bottom of the stairs. In their midst, Cheryl is bursting with delight. "Guess what, Madison! Smithy's on her way home! I talked to the headmistress and just got off the phone with Smithy herself. Smithy's on the train! She is so happy. She agrees that we're ready for a breakthrough. She can't wait to get here and be part of this wonderful forward motion."

You would think that the two deserting sisters would have stayed in touch. But what they've done is so wrong, they can't admit it to anyone—each other least of all. Madison, home at last, admits she's been looking for an excuse to come back. Dad's birthday and a stranger's Jeep sent the message she'd been wanting—go home. Of course Smithy feels the same.

But *this* excuse? All four children in front of cameras? Recording every sad, angry, mixed-up thought? Betraying their mother and father? Admitting how they feel (how *do* they feel?) about their baby brother?

She imagines Cheryl emceeing. Making sure her new wall colors are presented in the best light. Going to the mall, shopping for the clothing in which she will parade Tristan Fountain.

Madison wants to question Cheryl, preferably using instruments of torture. Are they paying you? Or is this so much fun that you're paying them?

The TV people balloon with delight. Today they will have their hearts' desire—two missing sisters within camera range.

The fat old phone below the large mirror is ringing again. Cheryl snatches it up. Immediately her face distorts with anger. "Madison said what? Mrs. Griz, I apologize for that. Madison has no right to interfere. Of course the producer and I will be there, just as planned. I'm so sorry about your conversation. Trissy's sister is at such a difficult stage."

Trissy?

Rhymes with "prissy" and "sissy"?

For the thousandth time, Madison wonders how God could let Cheryl live instead of Mom.

Cheryl covers the phone and hisses, "How dare you, Madison? You don't even live here!"

Mrs. Griz continues talking, so relieved she still has a chance to be on TV that she's shouting. Everybody hears her say, "I've alerted the staff and we're so excited!"

Rule: TV cameras are always welcome. That's where power lies. In television. It comes, it records, it airs, it lasts. A little boy caught inside television has nowhere to run. And there's nothing Madison can do.

Cheryl reenters the phone conversation. Her cheeks turn a

dull red. "Jack has already picked Tris up? Oh, yes, of course. How could I have forgotten that it's a half day?"

Madison assumes Cheryl does not have the slightest idea what anybody's schedule is, which is nice. If asked, Madison will also claim a half day as her own reason for showing up.

"Oh, goodness," cries Cheryl. "I'm glancing at my cell phone, and I see there is a text message from Jack. No doubt he's letting me know. I've been so busy with the television crew, I just haven't been aware of other details. Well, it doesn't matter. We'll still drop by. I have the associate producer and assistant director here."

Madison studies Angus and the bad-hair woman. Associates and assistants should be in their twenties, shouldn't they? These two are probably in their forties. Perhaps they are not as success-ful as they claim.

But that will not help, because people without success *really* want to present a riveting, heartbreaking family drama. And as far as television is concerned, the Fountain story has no missing ingredients. It will be a nice career move for these two.

Coming down, her eyes averted from all those stares, Madison gets a momentary glimpse of kitchen cabinets at the far end of the hall. Her mother was the cookie maven: chocolate chip cookies, peanut butter cookies, molasses cookies, iced cook-ies, spritz cookies. Her mother loved that kitchen. Lived there. Sang there. Danced. Wiped away tears and celebrated triumphs. Read library books and—

Madison is going to cry.

Slowly, as if capturing a wild animal apt to spook, the cam-eraman lifts his camera to his shoulder.

"Emotions are going to be very high," says Angus, this man whose emotions are probably like a cotton shirt, just something to wear. "You know what, Maddy?"

Only Mom called her Maddy. When Mom died, Madison never wanted that nickname again.

Angus trots out his smile. It's a rich smile, as if anybody he shares it with will become healthy, wealthy and wise. "Let's you and I both meet Smithy at the railroad station! After all, we can get the day care anytime. And without Trissy, it's lost any real meaning, hasn't it? But you—the beautiful sisters, your first re-union—is it your first reunion?—I mean, think of it. The beautiful moment when you start to rebuild your family, facing tragedy with courage because you're together."

They are beautiful sisters, and Madison has been dreaming of the moment in which she and her sister face their tragedy with courage because they're together. But not in front of a TV crew sniffing the air like dogs. "Gosh, it sounds like fun, but I have a dentist appointment. Bye." She walks straight into them, and they are forced to part. In a moment she's outdoors.

It's drizzling. The drops feel cool and good against her fever-ish skin. But the tenacity of TV is not slowed by a mere damp sky. The bad-hair woman follows so closely they could share a sweater. Madison cannot go to her car and she cannot call Jack.

• • •

Friday creeps by. Diana has a sense of being too late; of being wrong. It's a heavy, dark feeling. She's been wrong and late already today, wasting the entire morning before making the decision to interfere in Jack's life. The brief conversation with Jack's aunt Cheryl keeps repeating in her mind. Mrs. Rand was awfully excited about a paint event. And when Diana strapped Tris into his car seat, what was with the smug little smile? Even Cheryl can't gloat over clutter removal.

In spite of the fact that Cheryl's a big spacious woman, covered with attractively tailored clothing, adorned with well-chosen jewelry, she seems slimy to Diana. Diana thinks of her as a jellyfish floating on the surface, poisonous tentacles reaching down. Diana's mother disapproves of talk like this. "That's just plain mean, Diana. Where would those children be without Cheryl Rand?"

Better off, in Diana's opinion. Last winter, the older three were so stunned by their father's death and how it happened, they couldn't even stand up straight. They stumbled around, hunched and silent. Cheryl liked to remind Smithy and Madison that the reason they didn't have a mom, and the reason they didn't have a dad, was sitting right there needing a fresh diaper. Oh, you have a chance to get out of here? cried Cheryl. Take it!

When Smithy asked to move in with the Murrays, Diana was thrilled.

No, said Diana's mother gently. Life is tough, but Smithy has to stick it out at home. She still has a family, albeit one that is smaller and sadder. We Murrays will always be here for her. But Smithy can't move out.

Diana's mother was wrong.

Smithy moved out within days. Diana's friendship, the years

of dolls and ice skates, slumber parties and lipsticks, was over. Instead, Diana became that handy tool, the babysitter down the block.

"Cheryl has to be doing something right," her mother insists. "Tris is a great little guy."

Diana does not agree. What saves Tris is a great day care and a great brother.

Diana leaves her cell on, hoping Jack will update her. But when it rings during literature, the caller ID says Reed Fountain. Diana almost faints. Is he calling from heaven?

Cell phones are not allowed in class to start with, but talking on them is absolutely forbidden. People often text, holding the phone under their desk, and some people even manage to play games, but Diana is not in this group. She gives the teacher a tight apologetic smile, whispers, "Sorry!" and scurries out of the classroom. The teacher says something, but Diana chooses not to hear. "Hello?" she says into her phone. She's never talked to a dead man. She walks swiftly down the hall in case the teacher pursues her.

"Jack took Tris early from day care because it's a half day," says Cheryl in a taut, angry voice.

Diana reexamines the caller ID. It's the Fountains' house phone, hardly ever used. Cheryl always calls from her own cell. Cheryl has gotten rid of every other trace of Reed and Laura Fountain. She hasn't realized that the caller ID still shows up with the dead man's name.

In spite of the fact that it's Cheryl, Diana feels as if Mr.

Fountain is trying to tell her something. He's listening in, expecting something of her.

"Jack texted me," says Cheryl peevishly. "They're at a soccer game. But I *have* to pick them up, Diana. This is quite urgent. Who are they playing?"

There is no half day and the school does not have a Friday game schedule. They're not playing anybody.

But it is the plus and the minus of cell phones that the caller doesn't know the location of the other phone, so Cheryl does not know that Diana is still in class, and that Jack should be too. Diana backs Jack up. "They'll probably be home soon. How's the paint job going?"

"I can't start on that yet. I have other things on my plate. Di, I'm really worried. I need to find them."

She hates being called Di. "What are you worried about?"

"I don't know where he is!" cries Cheryl.

Cheryl Rand never knows where Jack is. Or cares.

"You know that Jack is very difficult," says Cheryl, who sounds as if she is crying. There seems to be somebody with her, comforting her. This is not good. Cheryl will do anything for an audience. "He keeps ganging up on me," says Cheryl. "I can't cope with him."

Cheryl is showing off for somebody, and she's doing it by slandering Jack. Who could that person be? Cheryl is friendless, as far as Diana knows. "I don't think one person can gang up on you, Mrs. Rand. I think a gang of people has to gang up on you."

"Fine!" shouts Cheryl Rand. "Don't help, then!" She slams

the phone down, which you can do with a house phone. Cheryl has a very expensive smartphone, and during television ads she watches videos, checks celebrity news and comparison shops. She wouldn't slam it around.

Diana wants to phone Jack, but what if he's in his room, rescuing his stuff? Diana's call will give away his position. No, wait. Jack can't be home, because he's got Tris. Tris does not have an indoor voice. He has only an outdoor voice. Cheryl would know all too well if Tris and Jack were upstairs.

Diana calls Jack, but it goes to voice mail. She is forced to leave a message. "Jack, Cheryl phoned me in school. She's hunting for you. There's something weird going down. Somebody else is in on it, but I don't know who. Be careful, Jack. Call if I can help."

• • •

"I'm Gwen!" cries the TV woman, jogging alongside Madison as if they're on the same track team. "Madison, honey, you're going to be a wonderful interview. You have so much personality. This program could open up a beautiful future for you, because you're articulate and sexy and full of character. Are you interested in the film industry?"

Is this the bait they offer Cheryl? She's "articulate, sexy and full of character?" That would be a hard sell, but maybe they offered that line to Smithy. Smithy, who crosses state lines to come home and blat on television about precious, private things.

Madison doesn't want these people to know about her car. A car is freedom, but only if it's a secret from the invaders. She trots

84

in a circle, heading instead for the backyard and taking the short-cut through the little woods to Kensington, the next street over.

"Where's your dentist appointment?" Gwen says. "We'll want to follow you during your everyday activities. Shall I drive you there?"

Even if Madison wanted to be on TV—especially if she wanted to be on TV—she would refuse to be filmed with her mouth open and her saliva dripping. The image is so preposterous that Madison giggles as she plunges into their neighborhood wilderness. It's not wide, but it is long. Chesmore and Kensington are separated for the length of the creek, with enough wetlands and rock-strewn woods to support turkeys, skunks, at least one raccoon and some years a fox. Jack and his friends used to play *Survivor* here, pretending to face danger in the forest.

Madison does face danger. But it isn't in the trees.

She avoids the path made by her father and Jack, because Gwen could just trot after her, and walks straight into the briars, letting them snag her jacket and trousers. Her sneakers sink into the little marsh, getting muddy and stained.

"Let me give you my cell number," cries Gwen, brought to a stop by thorns.

Madison hurries. Gwen is just the type to run all the way around and meet Madison coming out the other side.

• • •

Jack and Tris have no sooner finished watering a tree than Jack's cell phone rings. It's Diana. He doesn't even consider answering. He can't have a second conversation about Cheryl painting his room.

When Tris spots the big-kid jungle gym, he forgets the library and hurries toward the playground gate. Jack trudges after him. In adventure films, people soar with adrenaline and leap from cliff to cliff, using some vast, untapped reservoir of energy. Jack can hardly hoist his own sneakers. It doesn't bode well.

The phone rings again in his hand. He jumps at the sound of his own ringtone.

Madison. Twice in ten minutes. She sure is eager. How does television do this to people?

Jack answers carefully. One syllable. No inflection. "Hi."

"It's me, Madison."

"Uh-huh."

"I just drove over to the house. Jack, Cheryl's gotten hold of a TV producer. They want to do a special on us. On Tris, actually. They're going to bring in a psychiatrist and get us to talk in front of cameras and portray Tris as some evil baby creature, and hope that we cry, and above all they want to film the moment when Smithy gets here and we have a reunion. Smithy's agreed to this, Jack. She's in favor of it. She is actually on the train right now. She couldn't come home to visit us or anything like that, but a chance to be on TV, and she's on her way. Cheryl's trying to hunt you down for this reunion. She knows you have Tris. I called Mrs. Griz and tried to convince her not to sign on, but that's not going to happen. Mrs. Griz is going to help them."

The prospect of an ally should bolster him. Instead, Jack's

fading, like a setting sun. "How did you happen to be at the house today?" he asks, since Smithy isn't the only one who doesn't visit.

Tris reaches the jungle gym, stretching his little fingers toward the high bar. His pants fall down. Usually this means that Tris falls down too. Instead, he carefully pulls his jeans up. It's a first. Tris is normally as unaware of clothing as a chimpanzee.

Jack catches up and helps with the blue jeans. It's hard to hold the phone at the same time.

"I came home because of yesterday," Madison is saying. "Daddy's birthday. I'm the oldest. I should have gathered us together and bought a sheet cake, and we would have written I LOVE YOU, DAD on his cake, and had enough candles. Do you ever think of them in heaven, and they're looking down, and they're disappointed in us? Well, not you, they're not disappointed in you. But me." Madison is crying. Jack is oddly comforted by this. "There's a second thing that happened yesterday, Jack," she adds. "Mrs. Emmer had to go shopping at the mall."

Girls! Just when you think they have something to offer.

"I stayed in the car while the Emmers went shopping. I pretended I was going to study when I was really going to sit and think about Dad's birthday. And parked at the back of the lot was a Jeep. Same model and year as Dad's. I thought it might *be* Dad's, so I went over to look for initials carved in the dash. Well, there weren't any initials, it wasn't his, but it was unlocked. Remember how Daddy never locked his Jeep either? I couldn't help it, Jack. I opened the door and sat in the passenger seat."

He can't stand remembering this moment when their father made his final fatal move. Shut up, shut up! he wants to shout.

"Maybe not all Jeeps are like the one in the parking lot. Maybe there's something different about that particular Jeep. But here's the thing, Jack. The asphalt was flat and I knew the Jeep couldn't roll, so I tried to release the parking brake. I wasn't strong enough. It took me three tries."

Madison doesn't continue. She doesn't need to. She has just told him that Dad's death did not happen the way the witness claimed.

The only witness.

Cheryl.

It isn't Tris's fault? It never was? Is that possible?

But then how *did* it happen?

Tris's stubby fingers are wrapped around the highest bar, his little shoe flailing around trying to find the right step. "Don't help me," warns Tris.

Tris is like their mother. Determined. Now two weeks short of his third birthday, Tris has lost that baby look. He's sturdier and firmer. Like Mom. Sturdier and firmer in a decision than anyone Jack will ever know.

Jack has never cried. Not one tear. Not one sob. Not for Mom or Dad or Tris or himself. Now he can hardly talk over the lump in his throat. "We're at the library, Mad. Meet us in the playground out back."

• • •

Madison cuts through yet more backyards to return to her car. She hasn't run back and forth in the mud like this since she was young enough to play hide-and-seek. She's unlocking her car door when the windowless rear of the white TV van appears through the trees as it slowly backs out of her driveway. Madison leaps into the Celica, yanks the door shut and slides down as low as she can get behind the wheel. She's still visible.

The van heads toward her. Is Gwen driving? Madison doesn't risk a look. When the van passes, Madison straightens up. Tris's day care is in the other direction, so whatever the TV crew is doing, it isn't doing that.

Yet.

She starts the engine and is putting the car in first when the blue BMW drives straight toward her. It's Angus. Too late to duck—movement would draw his attention. She sits still. He's not looking her way. He's not looking at the road, either; he's fiddling with the windshield wipers or radio or something. The guy is a multiple menace.

There's one worry she can solve. She calls Mrs. Emmer. "Aunt Bonnie?"

Mrs. Emmer is always distraught when she's interrupted at work. "Hello, Madison, honey," she says, sounding frazzled before she hears a word.

"Jack phoned. He needs me at home. I'm just going to throw a few clothes in a suitcase and drive on over and stay for the weekend, okay?"

"Of course. Is something else wrong? Can I help? What shall I do?"

Madison is awestruck by Mrs. Emmer. What a sense of duty. How completely she has accepted her role as godparent. It

89

doesn't have God in it, but it has love. Maybe that's the same thing. "I think he's just feeling low. I've been the world's worst older sister. I'll let you know how it's going."

Madison heads for the library. It's only a mile. She checks her rearview mirror constantly. The three cars she's worried about—the gray Lincoln, the white van and the blue BMW—are distinctive. She doesn't see them and nobody is following her. Just in case, she goes through a bank drive-in lane, comes out in the supermarket lot and cuts through the alley, which is kind of fun. Or lunatic.

She parks behind the library. The children's playground is fenced so toddlers can't run out among the cars. Through the chain link, she sees Tris teetering at the top of the old-fashioned jungle gym, an open metal cube with crossbars. Her heart lurches.

But Jack is there.

Of course he is.

Jack lifts his big hands—hands that ought to be at football practice—as a net for his little brother. They both see her. Jack might be smiling. She pretends he's smiling. She waves, even though she's not sure Tris will know her at all, let alone from this distance. Tris waves back.

Waving is one of Tris's favorite activities, maybe his earliest. Talking comes late, and when Tris does start talking, he's comically adult. At two, Tris doesn't say "Me do it." Tris says, "I do it also." Tris loves the word "also." I eat a cookie also. I throw the ball also. I drive the Jeep also.

The media loved that sentence. "You do, Tris?" they baited him. "You drive the Jeep also?"

Tris would nod, eager to demonstrate.

Now Madison thinks, Why was Tris available to the media?

Because every time there was a camera, Cheryl put him in front of it.

•   •   •

The train seems to brake for miles before the actual station, wasting precious seconds when Smithy could be home. Smithy can hardly wait to get off the train. It seems that a friend of Cheryl's is visiting. He'll pick Smithy up at the train station and bring her home. His name is Angus. "I showed him your picture," confides Cheryl. "The really pretty one, when you were home over the summer and we went out for Sunday brunch. He's driving a blue BMW. I'm so glad you're coming home, Smithy! We've missed you so. This is simply wonderful!"

Aunt Cheryl has never written to Smithy. Never e-mailed. Never phoned. But who cares? All along, the family wanted her. Even Aunt Cheryl wanted her.

At last, the train stops and Smithy steps off.

It's one-thirty on the afternoon of November sixth, and her new life, or maybe her old one, is here.

A high wind sweeps away clouds and rain. The sky is clear and blue and immense. It feels like God. Are her mother and father somehow up there, in some space or sphere called heaven?

I'm sorry, she tells God. My baby brother needed love and I turned my back. I *have* the love. I just didn't use it. Help me go home. Let me love all of them. Let them love me.

The passengers head for a covered pedestrian overpass that leads to the parking lot. The stair is so high it's funny. Lighthouses have this many steps. Smithy is in the best shape of her life because boarding school is crazy for athletic activity. It feels good to run up, because this time she's running in the right direction. She dances across the walkway as the train below her roars out of the station, and then skitters down the other side.

A handsome man, with beautifully white hair and wonderfully blue eyes, is waving at her. His hair isn't old-age white; it's sun-bleached blond. What a great smile he has! This is Cheryl's friend? Smithy would have said Cheryl didn't have any friends, never mind a great-looking one like this. But Smithy has an attitude. She'll have to get rid of it. That's the point of coming home. Down with attitude. Up with affection.

"Your aunt Cheryl talks about you so much," he says, "I feel as if we're already friends. And don't worry about the whole school runaway thing. That can be solved with a few phone calls. How was the train trip?"

"Good." Smithy is so excited she's out of vocabulary. It's a neat feeling, as if she's all heart and soul. She's vaguely aware of somebody with a monster camera filming the station. Probably a promotional thing. Not that November is a great advertisement for tourism in Connecticut.

The blue BMW Cheryl mentioned is idling in the tow-away zone. Smithy darts over, and has to wait forever until Angus reaches his car. When he leaves the parking lot, there's an annoying intersection to negotiate where he'll turn left onto the

Post Road and from there onto the thruway. Angus leans forward, studying traffic. He turns right.

Smithy feels a bit of unease. The Post Road has red lights for miles. It's slow. Nobody would choose it over I-95.

Before she can tell Angus to turn around, he smiles at her. It's too big a smile. Smithy's unease deepens. Could he be Cheryl's boyfriend? Has he moved in? Will her welcome home be diluted by this man and his huge smile? What if he's become a stepfather to Jack? What if Tris calls him Daddy?

Smithy will be the outsider. The classic nightmare: everybody knows something she doesn't know. Everybody has alliances she doesn't have.

Smithy hates Angus now, which is embarrassing. Having just told God that she is all love, perfect love, she finds that her first thought is of hate. She laughs. "How do you happen to know Cheryl?"

"Cheryl and I plan to embark on a project together."

This doesn't sound like romance. What project would interest Cheryl, who is certainly not involved in civic affairs or studying for a degree?

"I'm a television producer," he says. "I have wonderful opportunities in life. Every month is an adventure. Cheryl and I have an adventure planned."

Cheryl? Adventures?

"What shows do you watch on television?" he asks Smithy.

Boarding school is a holdout against television. Study hours are enforced from Sunday through Thursday night, seven to nine-thirty p.m. Bedroom doors have to be open, and every student must be doing classwork. Computers, yes. Computer games or videos, no. Smithy can only tell Angus what she used to watch.

But he has moved on. He names several reality shows—a family with skillions of children, a family whose children have disabilities, even a family with morbidly obese children. "Tons of fun to produce. So much drama."

"Wow," she says, bored. She has never seen any of these. Smithy prefers cops, arrests and chases. It occurs to her that she can watch TV again, like a regular person. This is a nice bonus to coming home.

"I see a McDonald's!" cries Angus, as if he sees the skyline of Paris. "I'm starving. Let's hit the drive-thru. What can I get you?"

"Oh, nothing, thanks. I just want to get home."

"Smithy, I'd really love to get acquainted before there's a big press of people around."

What does that mean? The only people who will press around are her family.

He turns into McDonald's. "Smithy, I want to do a documentary on the brave and beautiful Fountain children. Madison was just over at the house a few minutes ago, discussing it, and your aunt Cheryl is on her way to pick up Jack. It'll be a portrait of courage and determination."

A documentary? On her? On Madison and Jack?

It seems extraordinary that Madison and Jack would agree. Jack even shut down his Facebook page last year, as if he could close off all evidence of being a Fountain. If only Smithy had been home for the discussion. She's missed so much. Thank goodness she's here now. She won't miss all of it.

She sees herself lifting Tris for a hug. This time, the cameras will capture Smithy as a good sister instead of a rotten one. Maybe she'll bake cookies, like Mom, and pour milk, and be the sister who keeps a home, not the one who abandons it. She sees Madison and Jack smiling gently in the background.

She thinks, I didn't bring any makeup.

Seven

"THAT'S MADISON," EXPLAINS JACK. "GO SAY HI."

"Madison?" repeats Tris, his interest piqued.

What does her name mean to him? How much memory does an almost-three-year-old have? Does he recall her fleeting visits? Does he wonder why she didn't stay?

"Hi, Madison!" he shouts, running toward her. He allows Madison to hug him but quickly squirms away. Tris has always been an efficient hugger: squeeze and leave. He doesn't leave this time. "You're crying," he says, worried.

She's not exactly crying. She loves him so much she's soaked in tears. "The wind is in my eyes," she fibs.

Tris is wearing a baseball cap. Baseball was their father's favorite sport. He'd have loved seeing Tris in that cap. Tris takes it off and gives it to Madison. "There. Now the wind can't get in your eyes."

He's going to be like Dad. Dad loved to give stuff away. She perches the cap on her head. "Thank you, Tris." Then she glares at Jack. "He's soaking wet, Jack. All the playground equipment is wet. It's too cold for him to be out here in that thin jacket. I don't suppose you have a change of clothes for him."

He glares right back. "The first thing you do is nag? Drive away if that's your best effort."

"Let's go in the library, where it's warm and his clothes will dry out." She's sorry to begin rudely, but she's right. This has been the case all their lives. Madison is right more than anybody.

"I know what you're thinking," says Jack, "and you are not right a higher percent of the time than I am."

"Feel his clothes."

"Okay, so they're wet. So you're right this time."

They're laughing.

"I'm not going inside again," says Tris. "I don't care if I'm wet."

"Last time you and I were here," says Madison, "you were too little to climb the library tree house."

"The tree house!" he says scornfully. "I can get up that in a minute!"

"Wow. Show me."

"Okay." He races on ahead.

Jack and Madison take up conversation as if they've never been separated; as if they last argued walking to the school bus this morning. "I need to apologize to Tris," says Madison.

"Don't. He doesn't know you did anything. He doesn't know there is anything. It's one reason I'm so mad at Cheryl about this television concept. There's a chance—not a good one, but a chance—for Tris to escape what happened. And here she is, setting it up so there's no escape. He'll crash into that accident all his life. When he's five and starting kindergarten. Eight and playing Little League. Out come the headlines. Each time it's going to kick him in the face. Somebody is going to step away from him. 'You're that kid?' they'll say."

Tris is pushing himself against the heavy back door to the children's room, but it won't open. He isn't strong enough. And what about the Jeep? Was he strong enough then? Could Cheryl—would Cheryl—really lie about such a thing? What kind of person would implicate a toddler?

Madison opens the door for Tris. He charges in. Also just like Dad. All forward motion, all the time.

The library is full of soft noise: terminals hum, librarians chat, pages turn, printers click. Tris does not pause at the temperature control panel placed too low or the adult computer terminal left on but not occupied. Even though Tris is the button master, he has a mission: to prove he can climb the tree house.

"I've been thinking about what you said about the brake," murmurs Jack. "But Mad, the thing is, if it wasn't Tris, then it was Cheryl. And she couldn't accidentally release a parking brake by accidentally reaching inside somebody else's car, accidentally brushing against it and then accidentally locking the car after herself."

"I agree. And if somebody causes the death of somebody else, and it's not an accident, then it's a murder."

The sentence comes rather casually out of her mouth. But her own word—"murder"—assaults Madison, rolling down on her with the weight of a vehicle.

When she walked away last winter, did she abandon her two brothers into the care of a murderer?

* * *

Angus Nicolson enters the drive-thru lane. Smithy just wants to get home, but she doesn't want to offend him. He's the producer. It's only a ten-minute delay, she comforts herself.

"What's your favorite photograph of your mother?" asks Angus.

Easy. The photo she uses as wallpaper for her cell phone.

In this photograph, Tris is a week old. Mom is in bed, of course. Dad is sitting next to her, leaning on the headboard, holding Tris. Smithy and Madison are also sitting on the bed, smiling at the camera. Mom has lived through it. She's fine, the baby is fine, everybody's going to live happily ever after.

Jack is standing beside the bed, and behind his sisters. He is elfin. Over the next few years, he'll shoot up a foot and turn into a completely different person.

Baby Tris is asleep. He's a sleepy newborn. He opens his eyes, checks you out, has his bottle, goes back to sleep. Such a good boy! everybody exclaims.

They don't say it now.

Smithy doesn't show Angus this photograph. She's never even been okay when Kate asks about the photograph.

Kate!

Smithy has forgotten that Kate exists. The world of boarding school—Smithy's universe since February—vanished from her mind. Kate, with whom she had breakfast twice this very morning, seems as remote as her grandparents in Missouri.

Angus puts his window down because it's almost his turn to place an order. A gust of cold wet wind envelops Smithy. "What'll you have?" Angus asks. He smiles his huge toothy smile.

She is suddenly, massively, creeped out. What is she doing in a car with a total stranger—a man who could be anybody, a man who refuses to take her home? A man driving the long way instead of the short way?

All of a sudden, he's not just a stranger—he's strange. This whole thing is strange.

A feature on the Fountain family won't showcase Mom the heroine or Dad the solid, steady great guy. It'll showcase Tris, baby destroyer of families. It won't be about beautiful people. It will be about raw pain. Hers. Jack's. Madison's.

It will destroy Tris.

Angus hasn't asked yet about her favorite photograph of Tris. She's got it on her phone too, and sometimes she can stand to look at it. Dad took it when Tris was learning to walk, a skill that consumed all of Tris's time and attention. He woke up in the morning desperate to be lifted from the crib, hardly able to have breakfast, eager to start. He circled the coffee table a million times back when he still had to hold on, and as soon as he achieved unassisted walking, his goal was the stairs.

For a toddler, stairs are enticing architecture. Smithy was the one willing to go up and down with him all day long. Tris didn't know that turning around was treacherous, that his little feet would not stick to the stair. Smithy was his main catcher.

Dad took a great shot of Smithy helping Tris down.

In no time, stairs were history. Tris ran, crayoned, wore little blue jeans with stitching on the seams. Smithy turned up the cuffs so he'd be fashionable. He had little baseball shirts and little train engineer overalls. When he began talking, he was such fun, Smithy could hardly stand it.

But to get Tris, they lost Mom.

Smithy thinks of this every day, sometimes every hour.

And every day, sometimes every hour, she thinks of her mother's final assignment: you and Madison be the best big sisters on earth.

Angus will want me to discuss that on television, she thinks now. That's the point. Crawl inside their little hearts and souls, scrounge around, leave them stripped and sobbing in front of the world.

"I have to hit the girls' room," she says casually, releasing her seat belt before Angus can end his smile. "Meet you in the parking lot." She's out, slamming the door behind her. Cars move forward and Angus has to drive up one. He cannot see her now and he cannot get out of line.

Also caught in the take-out line is a TV van. Probably even vampires like French fries.

Smithy darts in to find McDonald's packed with teenagers— not surprising, since Saybrook High is next door. She peels off her jacket, turns it inside out so only the white fleece shows and walks out with a high school group. It happens so quickly that Angus probably hasn't moved up a car length.

The teenagers don't notice her. They're laughing hysterically at nothing much, crashing into each other on purpose and high-fiving. She walks faster than they do, using them as a screen.

• • •

Tris proves how quickly he can climb, while Madison and Jack take a position behind the beanbag chairs. They are not invisible to the librarian—the library is arranged so that there is no such thing—but the staff pays no attention. They think nothing of two teenagers and a toddler early one Friday afternoon; home-schooled kids are here all the time.

"Say you're right," says Jack. "Say Cheryl did it. Why? What would make her do that?"

A TV cop show requires a complex, gruesome murder within the first minute. But this is life, where murder doesn't happen. Only breakfast happens, and then school, and you outgrow your clothes and watch a little TV, and your friends come over.

Madison has a hard time squashing a spider. She can't watch Animal Planet because some poor dog gets hit by a car or some little meerkat roasts in the Kalahari sun. And she and her brother are actually discussing the possibility that their very own father, the one they need so much and can never replace, was killed by another person?

Madison cannot think of a reason to kill anybody, never mind Dad. Furthermore, she isn't just postulating that Cheryl killed Dad. She's saying Cheryl blamed a two-year-old for it, thereby taking a second life—Tris's. And now, Cheryl plans to chop it up, burn it and make a TV show out of it.

"If we accused her, Cheryl would get a lawyer," says Jack. "The lawyer will point out that individual vehicles behave individually. Some Jeep in a parking lot has nothing to do with Dad's Jeep a year ago. I don't think the police ever investigated, you know. Nobody ever asked for Dad's stuff, not even his laptop and his briefcase. I have them in the attic over the garage. A real investigation includes fingerprints. If Aunt Cheryl had ever been questioned or fingerprinted, we'd know. She'd have whined for months."

No police investigation?

It occurs to Madison that in letting go, the police might have been trying to help Tris. Maybe the cops had little boys of their own and just couldn't go there. It's a little kid, they probably thought, wincing. Make this nightmare longer and deeper? Nah, let's drop it.

"Or Cheryl could shrug and say Dad goofed up," says Jack. "Didn't quite get the car in neutral. Didn't pull up the brake hard enough. Tris only had to touch it or fall against it. I wish we knew why Dad got out of the Jeep to start with."

"He was rescuing a stray cat?" suggests Madison. "Getting the newspaper? Or he dropped something? Or Cheryl did and Dad had to squat down and reach under the Jeep to get it?"

"But then Cheryl would know why Dad got out of the Jeep, and she's always said she doesn't."

"But if she could be a murderer, then she could be a liar, too."

They try to think of a reason for Cheryl Rand to lose every bit of control and decency. Why destroy the very person giving her a home and salary?

Before Cheryl showed up, by far the most difficult part of life was just getting to stuff. Every sport, club, group, play, activity and friendship required a car and a driver. The Fountain kids walked, biked, begged for rides, took late buses and were generally a pain in the neck to coaches, teachers and other parents. Dad hired housekeepers. None of these women worked out. They didn't stay or couldn't be counted on or did the wrong things. And they didn't chauffeur. Dad cut back his workday, but even so he could barely drop Tris off at day care and still pick him up within the time allowed. The baby spent half his life in a car seat, while Dad kept track of Madison, Jack and Smithy on his cell phone and drove all over town dropping one kid off, grabbing take-out dinners, eating on the run, picking up the next kid.

Call me Aunt Cheryl! cried this long-lost semi-relative, appearing out of nowhere.

Nobody was actually fond of Cheryl Rand. In fact, they were glad Tris was in day care, spending his time with people who were crazy about kids. Cheryl was crazy about the house. She had a great place to live and a good salary. If she wanted more money, she could have asked for a raise or found another job. She wouldn't have had to kill.

And if she'd been planning to kill, she wouldn't have chosen a method as iffy as a moving car. What are the odds you could even bruise somebody that way, let alone kill them? The chances are much better that the victim would just jump out of the way.

Madison slides into a daydream—not for the first time—in which Dad jumps out of the way.

"Maybe Dad decided to fire her," guesses Jack. "He told

Cheryl he appreciated all she'd done, here's a good-bye check, hit the road."

Madison can imagine Cheryl having been upset if she'd gotten fired. But upset enough to kill? "There has to be more to it. Maybe Dad found out that Cheryl was buying herself shoes with the money Dad gave her for the house. Or she locked Tris in his room so she could watch TV in peace."

Tris can tell they're talking about something interesting. He climbs down from the tree house. All interesting discussion comes to a halt. Tris looks at them suspiciously.

"Guess what I have in my backpack," says Jack.

Instantly Tris is excited. "What?"

"The fire truck!"

Madison even knows what fire truck it is. Nonny and Poppy brought it when they visited last summer—that awful failed visit when nobody made an attempt to talk to their grandparents because nobody knew what to say. The truck pops, sirens, squeals and grunts. It has red and yellow blinking lights. It needs four batteries. One is always dead.

Jack shrugs out of his backpack and Tris joyfully gets to work on the Velcro closure. Tris doesn't seem to mind how hard it is, he just keeps at it. Is this evidence that he did move the brake? Kept shoving and pulling until he got it to work?

Jack does not help with the Velcro. Madison would have helped from the start. In fact, she would have done it herself. At last Tris succeeds in separating the layers and looks up, face shining with satisfaction. Then he reaches inside. "It's not my fire truck, Jack," he says in disappointment. "It's a shoe."

"Oh, right." Jack pulls out two boots. Now Tris finds the fire truck at the bottom. "Go see if the batteries are working," Jack orders. "See if the truck can go all the way to the windows and back."

Tris sets off.

Jack rotates the right boot until the carved initials are facing him.

Madison catches her breath. "Are those Dad's work boots? You carry them around?"

He tells her about Diana's warning, how Cheryl was going to declutter his room. How he raced home to save the boots, or actually their contents, and overheard the docudrama discussion.

"Who cares about that? You have Dad's cell phone? Jackster, that's great! You know how many photographs he kept. I bet there are photos from the night before, when we went to that Japanese restaurant and Tris was so excited by the hibachis, especially when the chef set the oil on fire."

Their father adored his cell phones. He had a slew of them, always ready to try another model with another cool gimmick. He played games, surfed, texted, kept his date book and above all, sent pictures. When he was out of town—which was a lot, before Mom got sick—he sent pictures of the view from his hotel room, even if it was a brick wall; the headlines of the local paper; the building where his conference was; the restaurant where they did lunch; the gym where he worked out as a guest.

In return, he expected the family to send him pictures. Mom actually kept him posted on the progress of the sweater she was knitting for him—see how the sleeve is two inches longer? She sent pictures of the dinner he missed and the annoying school board meeting he was lucky to have skipped. Madison, Smithy and Jack flooded him with pictures. If somebody was in a game, the other two were there to send pictures. They took pictures of their library books and their homework, the friends who came over and the mess they made fixing snacks.

Their father's cell phone hasn't been used in months. It's run down.

Madison has the same brand and therefore the correct charger. She takes it out of her purse, plugs it into the wall and into Dad's phone. Tris drives his fire truck over her legs and she remembers the TV van and the BMW.

Madison suddenly realizes where they are going. To the railroad station to pick up Smithy. Who wants to be on television. Who is cooperating.

Eight

THE WIDE GRASSY EXPANSE BETWEEN MCDONALD'S AND THE HIGH school feels so familiar to Smithy. She can't remember ever being at Saybrook High. Probably it feels familiar because schools are often brick and grass is often green. Then she realizes: it's not the school—it's the running. It's her theme song. Things get bad? Run. Things get worse? Run again.

Her little brother is about to be damaged, and is Smith Fountain providing damage control? No. She's on the run again.

Smithy is falling apart. Her skin is gone, her joints dissolve. She'll be a pile of legs and arms, her separated heart beating by itself on the grass.

The high school kids hurry because they have a schedule— places to go and papers to write. And what is Smithy's schedule? Does she plan to hide out in a bathroom in the school building? For how long? And then what?

When her cell phone rings, she's filled with fear, as if this will be some sort of retribution. And it is: it's Kate. Smithy has more or less kicked dirt in Kate's face. After all Kate did for her—all Kate's parents did for her!—Smithy can't even be bothered to tell her roommate what's up.

She answers because she has to, and out spill words she cannot control. "Hi, Kate. Don't be mad. I'm sorry about all this. I was rotten. Oh, Kate, things are worse. I thought they were perfect. I thought coming home would be perfect. It was my father's birthday and I was thinking of candles and cake icing, and even though I was late, I didn't think I was *too* late. But Kate, something's happening. I don't even know what. I can't even ask Jack or Madison. I don't even know them anymore."

• • •

A boarding school has few secrets.

Smithy is wrong that her background is a secret. She doesn't face questions only because every other freshman is also new; they're all away from home for the first time, learning to be roommates and to act independently; learning to live in the middle of a perpetual slumber party and yet study far more than they would back home.

Roommates are knit together. It hurts Kate that Smithy did not confide. Yet Smithy hid less than she thought. Kate knows about the photograph on the cell phone and the larger one in its silver frame under the stack of sweaters. She knows that this Aunt Cheryl has not once phoned, written or visited. She knows that the distant grandparents never fail to phone and write, and that Smithy always lies and claims to be busy. She knows that the few times Smithy initiates calls to her brother Jack or her sister, Madison, they have nothing to say to each other, and yet they're not angry; they're just unable to talk. They can stay afloat when they are apart, and the thought of coming together makes them sink.

Kate has no parallel.

The only time she and her roommate do not get along is when Kate dresses for church. Smithy has taken the stance that if there were a God, he wouldn't have let these things happen. So there's not a God. But even though Smithy insists there's not a God, she's furious with him. She says bitingly on Sunday mornings, "You're going to church? To practice some stupid superstition? Waste your time as if some Great Power in the Sky cares about you? He doesn't care, Kate."

"Did your mother believe in God?"

"Yes, and look where it got her."

"Maybe it got her to a good place."

"Oh, shut up already! What's good about it? Her baby needed her. I needed her. Dad needed her. Madison and Jack needed her. God didn't need her!"

Kate is one of only four students in the entire school who goes to church. In previous centuries, the boarding school was affiliated with a church, and students had chapel daily. Now the chapel is just a quaint building they don't use but aren't quite ready to dismantle. Kate attends church in the nearby village. This annoys the school because church presents a scheduling problem. Sports and daytrips take place Sunday mornings. Rather often, the faculty speaks disparagingly to Kate about organized religion.

Every Sunday morning, no matter what the sermon is about, no matter what the verses of the hymns claim, Kate puzzles over the tragedy of Smith Fountain's family. What can it mean? What was God thinking?

But no matter that Kate is Christian, and believes in love, compassion and forgiveness, she is not phoning to see if Smithy is all right. She's going to yell at Smithy. Call her names. Demand an explanation for this betrayal of roommate rules. Make it clear that the whole free-ride vacation scenario is over. Kate is not going to be Smithy's alternative arrangement ever again.

"I'm practically a criminal," Smithy is saying. "I disbanded my own family. And I don't know how to get back in."

Kate tries to climb into this incoherent conversation. "Are they barring the door? Will they talk to you?"

"I don't know. I don't even know who they're talking to. I think they've agreed to it. But I'm not going along with it." Suddenly Smithy's voice is calmer. "I can't talk anymore, Kate. I have to get back to that car. I can't let them know that I'm on to them."

Kate has no idea what Smithy is talking about. "I called to say I love you," she says, a total lie five minutes ago and a total truth now. "What can I do, Smithy?"

Smithy's voice cracks. "Pray for Tris."

Kate is one of the few kids on campus this Friday wearing a good thick jacket even this early in the season. Inside her jacket she freezes up. *Pray for Tris.* This is a commandment from Smith Fountain?

Kate knows where the key to the little chapel is. They all know. It's interesting that there's been no vandalism to the chapel. Kate opens the building and walks in. It's dusty and very cold. It smells abandoned. Kate takes a pew, pulls out the kneeler. A bit of sun comes through dirty stained glass, like distant jewels. When she bows her head, the room feels full of long-gone prayer and song. Is it only Kate who feels this way, or is that why nobody has spray-painted graffiti or snapped off a carving?

God, she thinks, Smithy really needs you. I think they all need you. Especially Tris needs you.

Immediately she knows what to do. People who find church comical like to tell Kate she isn't "getting an answer" from God; she's just focused her own mind. If she comes up with a solution, it's hers, not his.

Kate walks out into the meager November sun. Stick with me, she tells God.

She makes a phone call.

●　●　●

Diana is in chemistry.

She and Jack are both in this accelerated science class. Jack is absent.

Jack loves chemistry. He's got a love affair with all his classes, and the energy he used to throw into sports now goes into study.

Jack has been an amazing big brother. Diana stands in awe of him. He has rearranged his entire life so that he won't lose the final member of his family. But since Tris is fine in day care, Jack wouldn't miss chemistry to take him out early. So something is going down. But what? And since Jack is lying about going to a soccer game, where has he taken Tris?

Not a mall or a store. Jack does not understand the joys of shopping. And Tris is a nightmare in a store—grabbing everything, wanting everything, cranky about everything. If Tris were a purchase, you'd exchange him.

The only friend's house Jack might approach is her own, and Jack would not interrupt her mother at work except in an emergency. Her mother wouldn't let Jack skip the rest of the school day, either.

Which leaves only the playgrounds or the library. It's drizzling, so Jack's at the library. Diana has her car. She can drive over. But if Jack wants her, he'll let her know.

Every step of Laura Fountain's saga took place when Diana and Smithy were still best friends. Diana always knew everything within five minutes of Smithy's knowing it.

Laura Fountain was having a fourth child. She and her husband adored children and wanted lots of them. How nice that just as the older three became teenagers, a baby would be joining the family. But there was something wrong, and it turned out not to be the pregnancy. Laura Fountain had liver cancer.

The poisons of chemotherapy would destroy the baby. But if Laura Fountain chose not to have chemo, the cancer would kill her before the baby was ready to be born. For most women, it's an easy decision: don't have the baby. Take the chemo. Live for your other three children. For Laura Fountain, it was also an easy decision, but her decision was: Don't take the chemo. Give the baby life.

You can't do that! came the cry. You're young. You have your life ahead of you. Your three children need you! Take the chemo!

Laura pointed out that the baby inside her was even younger and also had his life in front of him. And yes, her three children did need her, but even more they needed to honor the life of the little brother to come.

It got on the news.

Laura was beautiful. She got sick in a very becoming way, growing pale while her hair still gleamed. If Laura was in pain or afraid, it didn't show.

What would you do? Diana asked her own mother.

Take the chemo. I wouldn't think about it once, never mind twice, her mother had said.

Laura had to do some serious doctor-shopping to find somebody sympathetic, and the doctor she did find was only slightly sympathetic.

In school, kids brought up on talk shows believed that everything was their business. They actually said to Smithy and Madison (but not to Jack, who would have slugged them), "Your mother really isn't going to have an abortion?" "Is it true your mother will die because she's having your brother instead of chemo?" "Has she changed her mind yet?" "Are you making funeral plans?" "Do you really want a baby that's killing your mother?"

Stay away from it, advised Diana's mother.

But how? After school, the neighborhood kids always gathered in the Fountains' kitchen, where Mrs. Fountain served cookies straight off the cookie sheet and then played board games or video games with anybody. On weekends, Mr. Fountain could always be relied on for a ball game. If there weren't enough people for a real game, he invented one. He was never tired and always had time.

Now he has eternity.

Chemistry class seems just as long.

• • •

Madison knows she'll cry once she sees photographs of the very last night they were still a family of five. She does not want to cry in front of Tris. The pictures have waited all these months; they can wait a few minutes more. Tris hands a library book to Jack, but when Madison says, "I'll read it to you, Tris," he has to think it over. What does he see when he studies her? Does he see a total stranger? Does he see a sister? Does he know what a sister is?

Does Madison know?

Tris makes up his mind. Carefully, he lowers himself into her lap. His pant legs are damp, but he's still a warm comfy bundle. This is why Mom wanted another baby, thinks Madison. To hold him in her lap like this.

"Don't turn the pages for me," Tris warns. "I turn them. You just say when. Keep your finger on the right word, Madison, so I can read too."

"Okay. This is the word we're on."

"No, it isn't. You already said that word."

"Can he read?" Madison asks Jack.

"No. He has that book by memory. He always chooses the same ones."

*   *   *

While Madison negotiates over page turns, Jack gets a small foil package of Goldfish crackers from the vending machines in the front lobby. He tucks a Goldfish here and there around the upper level and windows of the tree house. He waits till the last page is read and waves the bag at Tris. "I hid six Goldfish. Can you find them?"

"Can I eat the ones I find?"

"Yup."

Tris races away, caroming off a picture-book cart but not noticing, slamming into the corner of a bookcase but not notic- ing. Like Dad, thinks Jack. Don't waste time measuring. Just go!

"Tris is happy," says Madison.

Jack is annoyed. She doesn't have to sound so amazed. What does she think Jack's been doing all these months? Keeping Tris miserable?

But he doesn't yell at her. He needs her. "Little kids aren't subtle. They don't pick up on stuff the way you would. They have enough hugs and snacks, and you read enough books, and play

116

enough ball, and they're fine. They're too busy to think about what's going on."

Is this true? Jack will always wonder. Does Tris, on some level, share the pain of his older brother and sisters? Very little children have no vocabulary, so they can't exactly have thoughts, can they? But they can have knowledge, even without words. What knowledge does Tris have? Does he too know despair and loss?

His little brother searches for crackers. Tris can't count yet, but he loves to throw out random numbers. "Nine!" he shouts when he finds a Goldfish. "Twenty-five!"

There's nothing more to say about an accident Jack and Madison didn't see and about which they can only guess. To call it murder is going too far.

Jack returns to the problem of the TV docudrama. It's almost quarter of two. Cheryl could be signing a contract this minute, giving the producer the right to be in their house, and in Tris's day care, and in Jack's face.

He feels like a runner who should have stayed on base. He's trapped with nowhere to run. He'll be tagged. He'll be out. In a normal game, he'd shrug. There are more innings and more at-bats, and for that matter, more games.

But for Tris, this is the only game. They have to win.

• • •

"Seven!" shouts Tris, cramming Goldfish into his mouth.

What would his life be like, Madison wonders, if we had agreed to go back to Missouri with Nonny and Poppy?

Madison and Smithy had been horrified when Nonny and Poppy wanted them all to move. They had lost their parents; now they were supposed to lose their house and friends and neighbors and graduating class? Jack refused for all of them. We'll be fine, he told Nonny and Poppy. Don't worry about us.

So the grandparents flew away and in minutes, Madison, Jack and Smithy separated, little tops whirling in their own corners of the room. They didn't talk at meals. They didn't talk in the morning as they headed for the bus. They didn't talk. Maybe Nonny and Poppy had held everybody's hands, and without them, hands never even extended, never mind got held.

The day after Nonny and Poppy left, Cheryl took Tris back to day care. But the school he always attended didn't want a child who put others at risk. Cheryl found more day cares. When she gave the child's name—Tristan Fountain—suddenly they didn't have an opening after all. In Madison's mental checklist against her baby brother, she added, Day care won't take him.

Suddenly it seems odd to Madison that the old day care—the one Mom picked—refused to take Tris back. Who knows better than a day care that two-year-olds pull knobs and shove sticks? That two-year-olds belong in car seats, not playing in the front? That adults have a job—not to let the two-year-old play with dangerous stuff? That if something should go wrong, it's not the fault of the two-year-old?

Madison has a thought as awful as the thought of murder. Her hair stands on end. It's such a ghastly sensation she has to pat it down, fasten it to her skull.

"Two!" says Tris happily, showing off his Goldfish.

Madison calls 411 to get the number for Tris's old day care.

* * *

Smithy fingers her cell phone. Her skills are not what they were. At boarding school, she saw everybody all the time and there was less need to thumb information.

Since Madison has a car, she could come get Smithy, but Madison will still be in school at this hour. Jack does not have a car. Diana does, but she too is in school, and Connecticut has an annoying law: no new teenage driver may have any passenger except family. The theory is that teenagers, desperate to impress one another, drive fast and carelessly while they talk, yell, joke and sing with their friends. Smithy definitely would. In fact, she can't think of anything she'd rather do, after she's back inside her family, than talk, yell, joke and sing with Diana.

But there's no friendship left. Even when Diana wrote, *Got my driver's license!!!!!!* Smithy didn't answer. She was angry at Diana, who still had a nice life. Nice parents, nice home, nice family, nice dogs, nice future. There was no way to reconcile all the bad stuff that had happened to her with all the good stuff still going on for Diana.

At least, in the trail of destruction Smithy left behind, one person isn't mad: Kate. And how about Madison and Jack? Are they mad?

She sends the same text to each of them.

Leaving home was wrong so I ran away fr bdng sch
2day. Creepy TV dude met me. What is story? What
team r u on? Lv Smithy

She turns around. Angus has pulled into a slanted parking
space that faces the schoolyard. Two slots away is that TV van,
recognizable by the antennae on its roof.

This is a town where nothing happens. There's no activity, no
crime, no excitement, no nothing. It's too small for its own TV
station. These people came from a distance. Is it a coincidence
that they are parked close to Angus Nicolson? And how about the
camera she half noticed at the train station? Is this the same one?

Circling to avoid being seen by the TV van, she comes up on
Angus from behind. He is sipping coffee and fooling with his
BlackBerry. Getting into this car with him is risky. But Smithy
has to get home.

Angus sees her and chortles into his phone. His cheeks pouch
out, squirrel-fashion, as if he's protecting a mouth full of chuckles. "Gotta go," he says cheerfully. He sips his coffee affection-
ately, handing Smithy a paper bag that smells deliciously of
burgers and fries. He himself has no food. Proof that he has no interest in McDonald's—his interest is Smithy.

In fact, she bets he's the kind who never eats food loaded
with unnecessary calories and probably considers fast food beneath his gourmet standards. Smithy loves unnecessary calories,
especially French fries. Especially with ketchup. It's been ages
since that blueberry muffin at South Station and she is starving.

But she doesn't take the bag. "Oh, no, Angus, *you* wanted that, not me. Go ahead and eat, I don't mind. Turn right when you come out of the parking lot and I'll tell you how to reach I-95."

Angus drops the bag on the car floor and changes tactics. "Smithy, you are a lovely girl. Such good bones. You are undoubtedly very photogenic."

Being photogenic counts. One reason the media fixated on the Fountains was that Jack is this tall dark sapling with heavy dark eyebrows and shaggy hair, so handsome. And his sisters look strikingly like him, yet without the heavy dark look; they are slim and golden like their mother.

"Yesterday I was looking at footage of the funeral," says Angus, making a sad face, a sharing face, a face that says he too mourns.

He doesn't say which funeral. Perhaps he's hoping she'll ask.

The funerals are very different.

When Mom got sick, she presented her children with the facts, the probable outcome and the time line. Then she laughed. "Doctors don't know any more than weather forecasters. Forget them. I'll have your little brother, take the chemo, whip the cancer, and we'll all live happily ever after."

But when the baby was a few weeks old, their mother crumpled. She had given all the instructions there were to give. All the encouragement there was to give. She had given Tris life. She was ready to go.

They were with her. It wasn't frightening. Behind her closed eyes, their mother slowly went somewhere else, while they stayed behind.

A few days after Mom's funeral, Smithy, Madison and Jack were back at school, busy as ever. They all studied an instrument (Smithy violin, Madison flute, Jack sax), and there were practices and concerts. They all played a sport or two and had a favorite subject—math for Smithy. They all got good grades.

And then it was Christmas.

How Laura Fountain loved Christmas. She used to start decorating the Friday after Thanksgiving. She'd haul out her CDs of carols and choirs, organs and bells, bring evergreen boughs into the house and unpack her angel collection.

Her last Christmas—before they knew about the cancer— Mom was in charge of Sunday-school crafts. She designed angels using large double-angled silvery paper clips. Each angle became a wing. A silver ball threaded on a slender ribbon was the angel's head and also the hanger for the tree. Most kids made a dozen, to hand out and slip in stockings.

Dad insisted that they could produce a Christmas worthy of Mom, who would be the angel looking down. It was almost fun making sure they omitted nothing. Not a CD was left unplayed, not a windowsill was without its battery-lit candle. They cried, and yet Christmas worked. Maybe because Christmas is about a baby. Jesus's life begins in beauty, full of shepherds and kings, angels and stars.

"What are you thinking about?" asks Angus.

"Jesus," says Smithy. She feels pretty sure Angus will not pursue this, and she's right. He sips his coffee and obeys her instructions to merge with turnpike traffic. Even at seventy miles an hour, he occupies the driver's seat as if it's a lounge chair. The warmth in his voice almost removes meaning from his question.

"Tell me," says Angus. "What was it like to realize your mother would rather die than bring you up?"

In the cup holder sits a tiny black recorder. It's on.

*   *   *

Madison lies to the director of Tris's old day care. "We're thinking we might bring Tris back to you," she begins.

Immediately it isn't a lie. It's possible. Can Madison return things to what they were? She's off to a good start: she's home again. Maybe she can put Mom's cookbooks back on the kitchen counter, Dad's sofa back against the wall.

"We would love that!" cries the director. "We were heartbroken when Mrs. Rand said she wouldn't be bringing Tris back. We were his family and we loved him so."

Madison's tongue dries out. It's a stale crust of bread. Words leave her mouth like dry crumbs. Even though she guessed this, she isn't prepared for it. "What reason did Mrs. Rand give for not bringing Tris back?"

"She said she'd be taking care of him at home. Months later we found out she put him in another day care. I almost called her up, but if Mrs. Rand felt more comfortable with Tris somewhere else, it was her call."

Madison is trembling. Why go to the trouble of finding a different day care when the old one wanted him back? After such a catastrophe—the loss of his daddy—anybody, even Cheryl, would want a little boy to have familiar loving adults around him.

"Tell me how Tris is doing," says the director. "There's so

123

much love in your family. Your mother was a courageous example. I'm sure it's been terribly hard. We've prayed for you."

Madison's chest feels constricted, as if she's running out of space for her heart and soul; as if the viciousness of Cheryl Rand is subtracting something vital. "Thank you. We'll talk later, okay?" She hangs up.

"Jack?" says Tris sadly. "Are we ever ever going to have lunch?"

Immediately Madison is starving. She's ready to throw the whole thing over for a hamburger. There's a Bible story about a guy who shrugs off his inheritance to get dinner. Madison giggles.

"And the funny part would be?" asks Jack.

She shakes her head. Hopeless to describe how Jacob and Esau could be funny. She says, "I've got my car. We can—"

"Drive to McDonald's!" cries Tris. He and Jack are big Chicken McNugget people.

Madison has a reality check. "I don't have a car seat."

"We can steal Cheryl's," says Jack.

Tris's little mouth opens in amazement and excitement.

"Just kidding," says Jack, who isn't.

At Madison's side, a tiny red light goes off. It is replaced by a tiny green light. They have almost forgotten their father's cell phone. It has recharged.

• • •

Smithy reaches into her wallet where she keeps the paperclip angel her mother designed for Sunday school. She holds it tightly in the palm of her hand.

Angus skips from topic to topic, hoping to get her started. She imagines him watching footage of the funerals. It's disgusting. He's disgusting.

At Dad's funeral, Smithy kept her eyes closed. She could not look at that casket, nor accept who lay there.

"It must have been so hard when your little brother was born," says Angus, all warm and compassionate.

Smithy gives him the party line. "Babies are wonderful." .

"I love babies too. I have a kid myself. Lives with his mother."

Smithy stares at her silent phone, willing Madison and Jack to call back.

"Will you visit your parents' graves, do you think?" asks Angus. "I was just there. It's a beautiful site."

This creep trespassed on her mother's and father's graves?

"Your aunt keeps flowers on the graves, you know."

This is so unlikely that Smithy gets her balance back. If there are flowers on the graves, they won't be from the children, either. Mom's knitting circle probably, or her book group, or the church dinner club.

Smithy claps her hands, because it seems a better move than wrapping them around Angus's throat. "Let's hurry. Maddy and Jacky get out of school at three, so they'll be home by three-thirty."

Her sister hates being called Maddy and Jack has never once been called Jacky.

But Angus follows Smithy's lead. "Maddy and Jacky have a half day at school. He's at a soccer game with Tris, and Maddy has a dentist appointment."

Angus sounds like a member of the family. Maybe he's been

filming for days. It sounds as if Madison is living at home now too, and going to their old school again. Nobody's told Smithy. But why would they? How stupid to text *what team r u on* to the very people whose team she quit. She's the one not on the team.

Ten minutes until she gets home. Ten minutes in which she cannot cry, cannot give this man a syllable. She begs Angus to tell her about his work. He goes into detail about a show where the children have dreadful, disfiguring birth defects. The surgical repairs leave hideous scars. He describes the special lighting they use so that these scars can be seen clearly by the viewers.

Angus—the man who will scar Tris for life—takes the exit for Smithy's house.

• • •

"You have any money?" Jack asks his sister.

Madison gives him a twenty.

"Wow. Do the Emmers give you an allowance?"

"No. Wade does. Don't you get an allowance?"

Aunt Cheryl gives him lunch money. But he doesn't have an allowance. There's no time to consider this. "Tris, we're going to get something to eat," says Jack. "Find your fire truck and drive it back here."

"Okay." Tris sets off. When he comes upon the fire truck, he forgets about driving it back to Jack. He's on his hands and knees, taking the corners hard, and yelling, "Fire! Get out of the way!"

Jack takes advantage of this gift of time to open his father's cell phone. He pulls up the first picture, which will actually be the last one Dad ever took.

At family events, like this night at the restaurant, they used to take turns with the camera, so nobody ended up left out of every photograph. There should be at least one of Dad himself. It's an unsettling thought. Will Dad look alive, waving like a living portrait in a Harry Potter movie?

But what comes up is not from the Japanese restaurant. It's a clear but meaningless picture of pale ridges, wrinkles, curves and a red spot.

"Fingers," says Madison finally, "making a fist."

"Cheryl's fingers," says Jack. "The red is her thumbnail."

"She didn't go with us to the Japanese restaurant," objects Madison.

Jack is puzzled. When did Dad take a picture of Cheryl's fist? And why? What came later than their final dinner out?

The next photo is also confusing. Blurry darkness with pale blobs around the edges.

Madison is laughing. "Tris's fingertips," she says. "Aren't they sweet? So it's Tris taking the pictures."

Jack's mouth tastes funny. He's losing the ability to breathe again.

The third picture is Cheryl's face, very close. Little clots of mascara clog her eyelashes.

He clicks. The fourth photograph is the dashboard of the Jeep. There can be no confusion about where the photographer is—the angle is from the passenger side, and slightly above.

So these photographs have to have been taken after that

dinner out. Taken by Tris. In the Jeep. There is only one time in his life when Tristan Fountain was standing up in the front seat of the Jeep holding Daddy's cell phone in two hands.

A cell phone not only stores pictures, it dates them. This one presents not just the day, month and year, but also the hour and the minute.

Jack is weak with shock. Tris was taking these pictures as their father died.

The fifth picture shows Cheryl through the Jeep window. No head—just her trunk. She's wearing the olive wool suit he suddenly remembers from that terrible day. Her arm and hand rest on the window, her ring catching the light.

The sixth photograph is at the Japanese restaurant, taken by Dad, because all four children are in it and Dad isn't. Not one child is looking at the camera. They are all distracted and unaware.

Nothing changes, thinks Jack grimly.

Now he clicks in the other direction through the five photographs taken by Tris. Timewise, he's following the action as it happened.

First, Cheryl is outside the Jeep, facing away from the house, toward the rear of the Jeep. Second is the dashboard photo, which places Tris inside the Jeep, standing up on the passenger seat. Third is Cheryl's face, inches from Tris. At this moment, she is unquestionably inside the Jeep. Fourth, Tris's fingers, proving who is taking the pictures.

And the final photograph, the one of Cheryl's fist—

Tris is back, face crumpled in despair. "My truck doesn't work."

Jack hands Madison the phone, forcing himself to examine the fire truck. It's not the batteries, because the lights and sirens are still going. He finds a pebble wedged under the axle that is preventing the wheels from turning. They probably brought the pebble into the library themselves, caught in the soles of a sneaker. He shows Tris the problem. "You be the mechanic."

Tris's little fingers work to extricate the pebble.

Madison holds the phone up for Jack to see. With her own long clear fingernail, she taps a point on the final photograph.

Cheryl's fingers are not making a fist. They circle around something. Cheryl holds it tightly. Its tip is dark and round.

It is the parking brake.

Nine

THE SIGHT OF ANGUS IS REPELLENT. SMITHY TURNS AWAY AND stares out the window on her right. In the exterior rearview mirror, she spots the white television van.

Angus flicks his turn signal and takes the off-ramp. Two cars later, the van also exits.

At the light, Angus signals a left. The van follows.

Smithy feels about five years old. She needs a hand to hold.

She has a sudden memory of Dad taking the four of them shopping. What was the occasion? They weren't in the Jeep, which wasn't big enough for the whole family. They were in Mom's car. (Dad always called it that. "We'll take Mom's car," he'd say.) Smithy sees herself getting out of the Suburban. She's wearing sandals, so it must be warm weather. She can hear the satisfying clip-clop of flat soles.

Who gets Tris out of his car seat? She can't picture that. But they let go of him. As soon as he can walk, and certainly once he can run, Tris is on the move unless you have him in a harness. He doesn't mind crashing into things so he doesn't look left, right, up, down or across. He just runs.

"Hold your brother's hand!" hollers Dad.

Was he yelling at me? thinks Smithy now. Did I hold Tris's hand? Or was I the one who let go?

Angus Nicolson swings into Smithy's driveway with the ease and confidence of a frequent visitor. "We're here!" he cries, as if it's Disney World. Like Aunt Cheryl, he parks so he has the fewest possible steps to the door. "Home again, home again!" he sings.

I'm not five, Smithy tells herself. And no matter what, this time I have to hold my brother's hand.

She does not get out of Angus Nicolson's BMW. She hardens her heart and puts a grim edge in her voice. She looks straight at him. "You film me and I will explain how you groped me. I will tell them where you touched me. I will tell the disgusting things you wanted from me."

Angus is not expecting this. He shrinks back, visibly calculating how this could damage him.

Smithy enunciates each word. "I don't want you or your people in my house." She opens the car door, gets halfway out, and gives her last command. "Call your camerapeople, Mr. Nicolson. Tell them not to step out of that van. They and you are not welcome."

• • •

The firecrackers in Jack's brain are bursting, but not with pain. It's more like the wild excitement of a Fourth of July sky.

131

These photographs are proof. They will stand up in court. They will exonerate Tris.

Tris did get into the front seat. He did play. But not with the brake.

It is Cheryl's hand on that brake. There's the unusually deep inward bend of the thumb joint.

We believed her, thinks Jack. We *all* believed her, all the time. Even I believed her! I went on loving Tris. But I believed her.

He's getting chills and aches from understanding what really happened.

But what happened afterward gives him a fever.

Jack is living with the person who caused his father's death. Jack has obeyed this woman. Gone grocery shopping with her. Put gas in the tank of her car for her. Smiled at her. Asked her permission for stuff. And as if that weren't bad enough, Jack has actually protected her.

The police didn't see these photographs because he, Jack, removed the evidence. He tampered with a crime scene. Cheryl didn't have to cover her tracks. *Jack* covered them.

His father's killer sleeps in his father's room. Successfully places the blame on Dad's baby boy. Spends the money Dad earned. And even gets a fine reputation as a good aunt.

He sees now why Cheryl has always been a little bit afraid of him.

Because if Jack only knew . . .

Well, now he does.

• • •

How glibly, how casually, Madison tossed out the idea that Cheryl Rand could be a murderer. Now the truth of it fills Madison's body as if she has cement in her veins. She is hardening. It is such a terrifying sensation that Madison reaches for her favorite lifeline—her own cell phone. She has a text message waiting.

"Smithy texted," she reports to Jack, and adds in a snide voice, "Smithy—who's coming home just to be on television." Then she reads her sister's message. Smithy is not coming home to be on television. She's just coming. Because it's home. And she is not on board with the docudrama. She's as upset as they are.

Yet another opportunity to know that she, Madison, is not the good guy.

The cement encloses her heart; there is no room for it to beat. She knows—she knew all along—that dumping Jack and Tris and Smithy was wrong. But the fact in the photograph—the fact of her brothers' caretaker as killer—is so huge that Madison does not see how she can rise above it.

How amazing that Smithy ran away from school the very same morning Madison found the courage to head home. Did each sister sense, at the same moment, that their family was again being threatened? Did a dead parent send a message?

But if a dead parent could do that, their dead mother would have sent Dad a message to get out of the way of a rolling vehicle. And if there were a way to communicate with dead or missing minds, Madison would get daily advice from her mother and father.

Oh, Lord, prays Madison. Can I still do something good?

She holds her phone for Jack to read Smithy's message.

"Why were we so sure that Smithy was coming home to be in the docudrama?" asks Jack.

Because I'm a bad person, thinks Madison. I leap to nasty conclusions. I don't have faith in my own brothers and sister.

Jack answers his own question. "Because Cheryl said so."

The list of Cheryl's lies is getting long. What else have they accepted, just because Cheryl says so?

Jack turns his wrist over. Like their father, he wears the face of his watch on the underside of his wrist. Madison also checks the time. It's two o'clock.

Madison is filled with dread. Cheryl is a brilliant engineer. She'll have a plan. Maybe she's always had a plan—maybe from the day she showed up, she had a plan. She's moving ahead with it, while Jack and Madison are bungling and stumbling.

We have to have a plan too. But what?

● ● ●

Home is where your mother and father are. Except in Smithy's case. She is reduced to her aunt Cheryl.

At the front door, Aunt Cheryl embraces Smithy, steps back to admire her, makes little cooing noises of affection and embraces her again.

Smithy peels her off. "They're not coming in," she says, gesturing at the camerapeople. "Go back inside, Cheryl. Shut the door behind you. We have to talk."

Cheryl hovers uncertainly on the threshold. She makes an error in judgment and heads for Angus. Smithy steps in alone, closes the front door and bolts it behind her. Immediately she's sobbing. "Mommy!" she wails, stumbling toward the kitchen.

Back Before, when Smithy came home from school, the destination was always the kitchen. The children always came in through the breezeway. If their shoes were muddy—Jack's were always muddy—they kicked them off outside the kitchen door and ran around in their socks. Food was always the plan. Usually it was waiting on the counter or coming out of the oven.

They played a lot of games in this kitchen—board games, card games, video games. Mom was also the art director. Crayons and paste when they were little, paint and beads when they were older. In this room, Dad and Jack went through a model train stage. Their enthusiasm didn't last, but the slab of plywood on which they fastened tracks and added a little town stayed a long time.

The kitchen is so empty.

Her mother's life created piles. Knitting alone meant old projects, new projects, half projects and swatches. Laura Fountain was also a reader, so books were stacked and marked and splayed open. She was a musician, so her CDs, tapes and ancient recordings spilled everywhere. There used to be mounds of concert programs and calendars and committee agendas. And always that faint dusting of flour.

The faded old sofa is gone. A small sleek couch is in its place. If there is such a thing, it's a one-person couch.

The big TV is still in the front room. Dad almost never went there. After eating dinner, and putting Tris to bed, and cleaning up, he'd lie on his sofa, using the little kitchen TV as radio, listening but not looking, letting a sports commentator be his lullaby. Smithy often snuggled up. Sometimes they didn't even talk. You don't always need to talk. Sometimes you just warm yourself by the fireplace of your dad's presence, and everything is better because he is there.

Tris will never know that feeling.

Smithy's cell phone rings. She can almost feel Cheryl's rage bouncing off transmitters on distant hills.

Worse, Angus will be over his shock. He'll be planning how to turn Smithy's behavior to his advantage. The camera crew is probably out of the van. Perhaps Angus is narrating into a microphone. The dear saintly aunt, in her struggle to keep the sad remnants of this family together, locked out of her own house by the—

But the caller is Madison.

Smithy sobs into the phone. "Madison! What'll I do? I'm in the house. I locked Cheryl out. The TV crew is in the front yard. I'm in here alone. Madison, it doesn't even feel like our house! Come and get me. No, don't! They'll just film us."

* * *

Yet again, Jack puts Tris's helmet on and straps him into the bike seat. Dunkin' Donuts will be warm. Tris loves donuts, and they can sit as long as they want.

Jack's route takes him past the empty football field. Incredibly, the school day is not yet over, so the team is not yet practicing.

His friends tell Jack, Leave Tris in day care. He isn't your responsibility. Let your aunt pick him up! Get back on the team!

They're right, and Jack has never been sure why he took on Tris like a permanent after-school job. Now he knows. At the back of his mind, he has known all along: this woman is evil. Jack cannot leave his little brother with her.

Jack misses sports so much his muscles ache. When he watches a game (Watches! How has this happened to him? How can he be a spectator, and not a player?), his hands feel the texture of the football, his toe pivots to change direction, his arms tighten to make the throw.

Baseball is his true love, of course. He's teaching Tris. They use a foam ball and a light plastic bat. It's pretty boring.

This whole season long, whenever Jack starts to watch a ball game on TV, he has to walk away. What good is it without Dad there to cheer and yell? Dad always kept up a running commentary on the plays—courteous if Mom was around to listen; swear words and vulgarities if she was not. Jack and Dad shared an easy conspiracy in their baseball attitudes.

Time is elastic. Time softened his sisters, and eventually Time will give him the sixteenth birthday he yearns for. But the time in which they can stop Cheryl is slipping away.

Suppose Jack goes to the police this afternoon with these photographs and his new explanation about how Reed Fountain died.

Suppose they believe him. The first thing they will do is remove Tris from Cheryl's care. They won't give him to Jack. Online (the only place Jack has ever done research), the worst stuff is the easiest to find. Jack has turned up hideous situations where foster parents abuse the children with whom they're entrusted. He knows most foster parents must be good people who love little kids. But life has already thrown Tris around. Jack can't risk letting anything else happen. Besides, online it says that the average stay in foster care is three years.

Tris would be six.

And suppose Jack goes to the police and they *don't* believe him?

Cheryl will have the ammunition she needs to put *Jack* in foster care. Jack can probably find parents of friends who'll take him in temporarily. Or maybe Wade will find a boarding school for Jack, too, and ship him out of state. Or maybe he'll end up in a juvenile detention facility where everybody else is a drug dealer.

Jack would survive any of that. But would Tris? Because there would be no Tris protection team left to prevent the filming of the docudrama and no big brother to stand between Tris and his own father's murderer.

Jack makes a quick detour into the parking lot of a chain pharmacy that has a large photo department. Once again, Jack frees his little brother from his child seat, fibbing about why they're here. Now he has to distract Tris, who will want to push all the buttons and examine all the photos. "Down this aisle?" he says to Tris. "Toys. Candy. Pick one of each. I'll meet you at the checkout."

Please don't anybody kidnap him right now, Jack thinks, jogging over to the self-service photo counter. The procedure is fast but takes a lot of steps. Jack makes mistakes. He's sluggish from the shock of Cheryl's lies and actions. While he's waiting, he downloads the pictures to his own e-mail, to Madison and Smithy and, after some thought, to Wade.

For a long time he had the idea that Wade was the guy's first name. It's actually Mr. Wade, a classmate of Dad's from college who does not live nearby. He was executor of Dad's will, and the judge appointed him trustee of the money. Now he will be the trustee of something else.

Jack takes a white envelope from the pile on the counter, slides the prints in, seals it and puts it into his backpack along with the boots.

Wait.

If the photographs are not sufficient evidence, Jack can't just give up. Obviously, his next move is to find more evidence. Not only has he never looked in Dad's cell phone before, he's never looked in Dad's laptop or briefcase. He didn't save these for their content—he saved them because he saved everything that was Dad's.

There's got to be a reason Cheryl took a terrible risk and did a terrible thing. Can there be a virtual or paper file or clue?

Tris tugs at his pant leg. His little brother has chosen Cheetos, which Cheryl never buys because they turn his fingers yellow. Cheryl never lets him have anything that will render him sticky, which is practically every food out there. Tris's normal state is sticky. For his toy, Tris has picked out a set of tiny metal cars enclosed in heavy plastic. Big print says "Ages five and up."

"Fine," says Jack.

* * *

How calm and reassuring Madison's voice is. Smithy hasn't heard it in so long. It's like really good music.

"Go straight out the back door, Smithy. I've got my car. I'm coming for you. I'm at the library, so I'm just a mile away, it'll take me only a few minutes. Go through the woods and I'll meet you on Kensington. So far today Jack and I have each run through the woods, so those people are used to it; they figure we're nutcases who are always thrashing through thorns. Don't look behind you. There's no video value in the back of somebody's head. I can't stay on the phone with you. It would be too crummy to get pulled over for talking on my cell while driving, and what else do the police in this town have to do?"

Smithy is out of the house like a shot. She's halfway across the wet grass before the glass door of the breezeway slaps shut behind her. She races toward the path Dad and Jack made so many years ago, in that other life. Are the TV people laughing at her? Will Smithy's role in this horrible documentary be her backside as she gallops like a cow across a pasture? "Mad, I can feel them back there snickering."

"They don't matter," says Madison, which is the lie of the century. TV always matters.

Smithy is into the trees. Madison disconnects. I won't cry, Smithy tells herself, but she's been crying since she entered the kitchen. She has to use her sleeve to mop her nose. She slips in the wet underbrush, scrambles to her feet mud-streaked and bruised and slips a second time.

She can see where Jack went through—the thin roller mark of his bike tires—and geometric sneaker prints that may be Madison's. The skid marks are her own. The neighbor is not going to be happy. On the other hand, the neighbor is not the outdoor type and with any luck, he won't come down here till spring.

Smithy staggers up the slope from the little wilderness and comes out on Kensington. It's a civilized street, with careful landscaping, symmetrical shutters and sealed garage doors. Smithy yearns for a life like that: neatly arranged, tidy and predictable.

Down the block, a car flashes its headlights.

•   •   •

Jack's phone rings. There's no law against speaking into your cell phone while riding your bike. He flips it open.

It's Cheryl Rand.

Can he speak to this woman? Should he? Holding on to his waist is the little boy Cheryl orphaned and blamed.

We don't have a plan yet, Jack thinks. We still need time. We haven't even collected Smithy yet. I have to keep pretending that nothing's happening, because the instant I admit that I know, Cheryl will head in some direction that I can't control.

Not that Jack can control any direction anyway.

"Hello, Cheryl." He's amazed how even his voice sounds.

It's the first time Jack has omitted the word "aunt." It's liberating. The courteous acknowledgment of kinship is over. She's not his aunt. She never was. She's a predator.

There's a pause, which is not like Cheryl. Either she notices he's not calling her aunt or she's got witnesses and is choosing her words carefully. "Jack, honey," says Cheryl.

She's got witnesses.

"It was wonderful of you to pick up the baby and take him to the soccer game. But it's been raining on and off all day. I'm worried that he might catch a chill. I'll come get you both."

Jack has a brainstorm. "Valley," he says. Valley Regional High School is a thirty-minute drive. "I'll meet you in half an hour at the front door." He disconnects, and notices Diana's message waiting. He listens to her offer of help.

They reach Dunkin' Donuts. Jack gets Tris down, removes both helmets, locks his bike and takes Tris into the warmth. His parents were big coffee drinkers who ground their own beans. The rich, coffee-scented air brings back the image of his mother brewing coffee, his father adding milk, the clink of spoons, the texture of bathrobes.

"You be the big boy," Jack tells Tris, loud enough for the counterpeople to pick up their cue and smile. "You order the donuts, okay? I'll find the seats."

Tris is excited by this responsibility. He lets Jack have his plastic bag with the Cheetos and the toy cars so that he can carry the donuts.

Jack is already finding speed dial, already sliding into a chair.

The woman at the counter leans way over to see Tris. "Hi," she says. "What's your name?"

Nobody ever figures this out, because Tristan is a rare name. This conversation is good for a whole minute, especially because the woman has a heavy accent—Spanish is Jack's guess—and she is going to have trouble with Tris's speech under any circumstances.

Jack is lucky.

Diana answers immediately.

* * *

Madison turns down Kensington. There's Smithy, at the far end of the long block.

Smithy and I came home because of Dad's birthday. Because we failed to celebrate it. In the end, there's only one celebration Dad would want—for us to be a family again.

Madison has always felt that without parents there is no family.

Now, she thinks, we'll always be orphans. But we can still be a family.

Madison stops the car, steps out and embraces the pale, thin, muddy girl who is her sister. "It's okay," she says, kissing Smithy's cold cheek. Unlike Madison and Jack, Smithy has grown no taller this year. She feels little in Madison's arms. Needy and scared. "It's going to be okay," Madison repeats.

Smithy lifts a tear-streaked face. "You think so?"

Madison's heart soars. She is the big sister again. "I do. Now get in the car, quick, before those TV people drive around the block."

"I'm muddy. What about your upholstery?"

"My upholstery is dying for evidence that my sister is sitting on it. Anyway, I threw an overnight bag into the backseat when I left the Emmers'. We're going to meet Jack and Tris at Dunkin' Donuts so we can talk. You can change into my clothes in the bathroom. Don't cry. It's okay. We're together."

"It's not okay, Madison. The TV people are right there in our driveway, and I made it worse. This man Angus—"

"I met him. He's a piece of work."

"Well, he's furious with me now and he'll be against us, and against Tris, and now the docudrama will *really* be horrible, and where are we going to go after we have a donut? Even Dunkin' Donuts doesn't let you spend the night."

"They haven't gotten us yet, Smithy. They haven't gotten Tris, either. We're still ahead."

Smithy takes a hunk of tissues from a little box balancing precariously between the front seats. She flips open the mirror behind the visor to inspect the mud damage, and moans.

"So listen up," says Madison. "There's been a development."

• • •

Diana is in her last class. The final class on a Friday is often a dud, but not today. It's political science, and in early November,

144

with elections only hours off, the class has a lot to contribute. When Diana's cell rings, everybody else is irked, because *they* remembered to turn *theirs* off.

Diana gives the teacher a snarky fake smile, and stage-whispers, "Have to go to the bathroom." This is an obvious—in fact, audible—lie, because everybody heard her phone ring. But at the tail end of the school day, the teacher is tired of the whole cell phone war. She waves Diana out into the hall as if swatting a mosquito.

It's so close to the end of class she might as well head for her car. "Jack?"

"Diana, I need you to do something for me. Please. I've gotten Cheryl out of the house. She's going to Valley because she thinks Tris and I are at a soccer game there. While her side of the garage is empty, I need you to pull down the attic stairs and go up and get Dad's laptop and briefcase. If her car's there, you can't get the stairs down, so you won't be able to do it. I don't want Cheryl to know the stairs exist, never mind that the laptop and briefcase exist. Can you do it? Right now? There isn't much time."

Diana is attracted to this. It sounds both criminal and adventurous, but with nothing bad actually happening. However, Diana is a careful person—the perfect babysitter; probably the perfect future assistant principal. "What's the rush? She'll go shopping the minute you and Tris get home anyway. She'll be out of the house and you can get it yourself."

There's silence. Is Jack deciding whether to confide in her? If Jack doesn't trust Diana, he doesn't trust anybody, because only Diana stood by him and Tris all these months.

She reaches her locker, gets her coat, stocks her book bag and feels for her car keys.

At last Jack speaks. "Painting my bedroom is just icing on Cheryl's cake. Her actual plan is a TV special about Tris. She's sold him to television. They want to do a multipart docudrama about how my mother died to give Tris life, making him a killer once, and how my father died because of Tris, making him a killer twice. She wants the house perfect for TV. That's what the paint job is about. She's got a producer at the house right now."

I'll kill her, thinks Diana. I'll entice her into the garage and— oh, what a shame, how could those attic stairs drop on her skull?

Jack isn't finished. "Madison and Smithy came home today. It's good because we've got a bigger team, but it's bad because we're the exact cast that TV wants to expose."

Madison and Smithy are home! Diana is laughing and thrilled. She trots toward her car. This is the best!

"Diana, when you told me Cheryl wanted to clear out my closet, there were things I had to get home and save. Dad's wallet and sunglasses and watch and cell phone. They matter to me, but at the same time, I never really thought about them. I recharged Dad's cell phone. There are photographs on it. Tris wasn't playing with the brake in the front seat, he was playing with Dad's phone. He photographed Cheryl as *she* released that parking brake."

Diana halts. She cannot both walk and grasp this information.

"Tris didn't do it, Diana. Cheryl did. There *is* a killer. It isn't Tris. I have proof."

This vision is so grotesque that Diana can't use an ordinary voice. "Call the police, Jack," she whispers.

"No! Diana, do not call the police! We are going to keep Tris *off* the news, not *in* the news. Promise me."

Diana doesn't make promises without consideration. She needs to weigh the pros and cons, consult with her parents, study the situation from various angles. But Jack has already broken the connection, and if she's going to get the laptop and briefcase for him, it must be now, while Cheryl is hurrying to the wrong location.

Diana reaches her car. She has to sit for a minute before she can actually drive. She just got away with skipping class. Has Cheryl Rand gotten away with murder?

●   ●   ●

Jack swallows bile. Saying out loud what Cheryl did has turned his insides to acid. He's shaken to find his little brother standing right there. How much of this did Tris hear?

But Tris is used to a brother who is constantly on the phone; he isn't wondering what Jack's talking about. He's swaggering with importance. "What kind of donut do you want? We have to tell Raquelle. She doesn't pick it out for us." Tris hauls on Jack's hand. "Jack, lift me up! I want to see the donuts too."

Jack cannot eat a donut. His guts will dissolve. He cannot be patient either. In spite of the fact that he's doing all this for Tris, it would be a lot easier without him.

God, he thinks.

It isn't a prayer, it's just a syllable, but maybe God thinks of it as a prayer, because immediately Jack has patience. He flips his brother in an airborne circle, which causes Tris to shriek in delight, and holds him up over the donut counter like a trophy. The donut selection is too great. Tris can decide between two things, but not fifteen. "You like chocolate icing," Jack reminds him. "How about chocolate icing with sprinkles?" Tris likes to pick these off one by one, using up lots of time and spreading chocolate over most of his body.

It occurs to Jack that the producer may still be at his house even if Cheryl isn't. TV shows love neighbors, they're always interviewing neighbors. They'll rush right over to film the adorable black-haired, blue-eyed neighbor stealing from the attic stash.

He almost smiles. Diana is one member of the Tris protection team who will never buckle.

"Raquelle, I like that donut right there," says Tris. "Please? No. Not that one. The one next to it. The fat one."

Raquelle puts the exact right donut in a little bag for Tris, who loves to carry bags. He loves to open them, peer inside them, take things in and out of them. In a few weeks he will be three. Who will organize his birthday party? Angus Nicolson, giving him a terrible fame? Or Jack and Smithy and Madison, giving him armloads of gift bags to open and enjoy?

Jack is unable to picture this birthday party, or where it would be, or who would come.

Jack gets a jelly donut, too. These will keep Tris going for a long time. Then Tris will be sick from all that sugar, but hopefully he won't throw up until they're outside.

• • •

Diana drives past the Fountain house. No cars in the driveway. No way to see if Cheryl's car is in or out of the garage. Diana doesn't want her own mother to see her, because Mom's favorite moment of the day is when Diana gets home from school and they have a snack and Diana tells her everything and Mom goes back to work all cheerful and restored. Diana wouldn't normally show up till three-thirty or even four, so her mother isn't keeping an eye out yet.

Diana doesn't want to tell her mother about the cell phone photos until she's seen them herself. She's already skeptical. There must have been a police investigation. They would have looked at every possibility. And when Diana does tells her mother, her mother will call her father, and the two of them will hash it out. They are practical people. They will call the police no matter what Jack wants.

Diana's hope in life is to be less practical than her parents. Maybe that's why she's going into the attic for Jack. There's a certain romance to it. Girl next door—actually, two doors—searches dusty attic for handsome boy.

Diana parks in her own driveway. Mom's office is in the back, so as long as Diana doesn't go in, Mom won't know she's here.

Diana walks down the sidewalk and past the Fountain house.

If Cheryl is still home, and if she looks out the front window and sees her, Diana will explain that she's located Jack and Tris; they're at Valley, in desperate need of a ride. Better hurry.

She circles the garage and peeks in the side window.

Laura Fountain's Chevy Suburban, rarely used since Cheryl rarely has more than two passengers, sits in its half of the garage. Cheryl's space is empty.

Diana has a key to the front door because she so often babysits, but first she circles the garage. The breezeway door is open. Jack probably lets himself in and doesn't lock up again, and Cheryl doesn't think to check. From the breezeway, Diana enters the garage.

Usually there'd be a long cord dangling here for pulling the stairs down. But Jack has removed the cord so that Cheryl will have no clue as to the existence of the stairs. Diana brings over an aluminum stepladder that's leaning against the side wall and positions it below the stairs. She climbs up and grips the little handle Jack has screwed into the stair panel. But the stepladder is now in the way, just as the car would have been. There's no space to lower the stairs.

She basks down and repositions the stepladder. Now she's too far away to reach the knob.

On a workbench along the back wall, Diana finds a short bungee cord, probably for fastening luggage. She repositions the ladder, hooks the bungee cord around the knob, backs down while hanging on to the cord, kicks the stepladder out of the way and hauls on the cord. The stairs are spring-loaded and don't want to descend. Diana finally gets them low enough that she can stretch up and grip the rim with her fingertips. She breaks a nail.

She is not in a good mood. When she pokes her head into the attic, it's pitch-dark, and although she fumbles in all the logical places, she doesn't find a light switch.

Sweaty, dusty and irritated, she descends and scours the workbench for a flashlight. No surprise: the batteries are dead. She opens drawers until she finds a pack, replaces the batteries and stomps back up.

Illuminated by the narrow swath of light are dozens and dozens of cardboard boxes, which Jack has labeled in a thick dark marker. *Mom's unfinished sweater. Dad's geodes. Mom's dessert cookbooks. Dad's ski jackets.*

Jack has rescued everything Cheryl threw in the garbage, as if he believes his mother and father will one day show up and need something to wear and stuff to do.

* * *

Jack opens a little plastic bottle of chocolate milk for Tris, who immediately knocks it over. Chocolate milk floods the table, Tris's lap and the floor.

It's too much. Jack cannot deal with yet another situation.

Before either Tris or Jack can cry, Raquelle is beside them. She stands Tris on his chair, mops him up with a little white towel and dries him off, chatting in Spanish, and Tris is laughing, as if he understands her.

151

Jack, too, feels better, because Raquelle is offering comfort— a universal language, although one that Cheryl Rand does not speak.

• • •

Cheryl Rand is halfway to Valley Regional High when she has second thoughts. She telephones the school office and asks for information about the soccer game.

Ten

EVERY SENTENCE MADISON DELIVERS IS LIKE A BLOW FROM A BOX-
ing glove. Smithy actually ducks. "Cheryl did that?" Smithy
wanted to think about home. About beautiful things like
Thanksgiving and Christmas. She expected to find them here,
like packages on the doorstep. Instead, she finds that her very
own father was killed on purpose—by Cheryl?

"I was just there, Madison. Cheryl touched me. Right here,
on my cheek. I've got her perfume on my skin. Madison, I have
to take a shower."

"You'll have to settle for the change of clothes I brought."

"They'll be too big. You're much taller than I am. I hope you
didn't choose your old retro baggy stuff."

"You'll live," snaps Madison.

They try to giggle about their quick return to bickering.
Instead, they touch fingertips between the seats. "Did you keep
your postcards, Mad?" Smithy asks.

"Jack kept them for me."

"I left mine at school."

"You can read mine. I'm sure they're the same."

The same is good, because now Smithy knows why Nonny writes the same four words every week. Because every week *Love you* is all that matters.

I'm home because of love, thinks Smithy. I was on the way home before I knew that Tris is innocent. I loved Tris again when the evidence was still against him. I can say, and it will be true, that I love my brother no matter what.

She weeps not for the evil that's been done to them, but for the light she has seen.

Jack consents to a replacement chocolate milk but draws the line at another donut. "No more sugar, Tris."

It's so weird to be the person deciding what's nutritious, because every food Jack likes isn't. So far Jack has never said "Now eat your vegetables," but he can feel it coming.

A silver Celica pulls into the parking lot. His sisters get out.

Madison strides in, wearing her take-charge look, the one that annoys Jack. She's wearing a twill jacket with still lapels, as if coming from an office job. She looks very mature. Since they no longer attend the same high school, and he doesn't see her, it has not sunk in: Madison is a senior. She must be applying to colleges. She must be doing it alone, or with the Emmers.

It's such an awful thought—Mom and Dad not here to take their oldest child on a college tour. Jack can't even manage a smile of greeting.

Smithy approaches slowly. Jack recognizes that look. It's a

cafeteria look. A the-tables-are-all-full look. A do-they-really-want-me-here? look.

For Tris, sisters are rare. They show up once or twice a year, not once or twice a day. "Hi, Madison," he shouts. "We're over here!" Then Tris recognizes his other sister. "Smithy?" he asks, looking at Jack for confirmation. Jack nods. "Hi, Smithy! Are we going to your soccer game? Did you already play? Did you win? Did you fall in the mud?"

· · ·

Smithy recognizes the denim-blue cotton sweater Tris is wearing. It's Jack's, knit by Mom.

When Tris was a few days old, Mom had Smithy go through the boxes in which Jack's baby clothing was stored. She wrote a list of what must still be purchased for baby Tris. Her hand shook. Weeks later, when they got to a store, they couldn't read the list.

When Mom was actually doing all that knitting, Smithy was irritated. Other moms were accountants and shop owners, doctors and UPS drivers. Mom just knit, baked, chaired a few committees and knit some more.

The other thing Mom did a lot of was church. For Mom, God was a distant second. She loved church for her friends, her committees and choir and the Christmas fair for which she knit so many pairs of mittens. When Mom got cancer, she added prayer to her life. Not for herself, she prayed for the baby.

Smithy detests the whole concept of prayer.

Tris's face and sweater are smeared with chocolate. He squirms down from his seat to come greet her, his sister who abandoned him. Prayer leaps in Smithy like sunrise. Thank you, God, for Tris.

She has the privilege of wrapping her arms around a baby brother who is glad to see her. Tris wriggles free and hurries back to give Jack a full report.

Smithy sits opposite Jack. It's all she can do to get a single syllable out. "Jack," she manages.

He nods.

Smithy slides her hand across the sticky table toward her older brother. Jack takes it. Then he tilts her hand sharply upward and they arm wrestle. Jack is so big now, it's like wrestling with Dad. Jack even has a shadow of a beard, like Dad. Smithy loses, but not really, because Jack is smiling at her and she is smiling back.

Madison buys chocolate milk and jelly donuts for herself and Smithy and sets them on the table.

"Cheers!" says Tris, raising his milk.

Smithy giggles. "Cheers!" They clink jugs. Plastic doesn't clink well but Tris is satisfied. "Where did he learn that, Jack?"

"The Murrays. He has dinner over there a lot."

How will Smithy face Diana, whose friendship she threw away like so much crumpled paper? Smithy looks to food for comfort and frowns at her donut. "Jelly?" she says to Madison. "You know I only like cream-filled."

They glare at each other.

"Then can I have your donut?" asks Tris excitedly.

They can all see that Jack is irritated.

"No?" asks Smithy doubtfully.

"I just told him he's had enough donuts," says Jack. "Oh well. This is different, Tris. This is Smithy's donut. You can have a bite."

Tris's face clears. He squeezes the donut until the jelly spurts out. Then he pulls the donut apart to see how much jelly is still in there.

"What made you come home, Smithy?" Jack wants to know.

It's a test question. The one with the most points and the biggest chance for failure.

"There was an assembly to talk about Thanksgiving plans. I was already upset, because of Dad's birthday. I wasn't home, and I didn't call home, and I sat there in that assembly realizing I don't even have a home. I have to borrow one from Kate. So I had to get back here in time for Thanksgiving and say I'm sorry." Smithy takes a deep breath. "I'm sorry, Jack. I'm so sorry."

Tris is wide-eyed. "Did you do a bad, bad thing, Smithy?"

"I did a bad, bad thing."

"Me too," says Tris.

If Tris says this to Angus Nicolson, the TV crew will go berserk with joy. They will insert these words where they have the cruelest impact.

"I spilled my chocolate milk," explains Tris. "Raquelle cleaned it up." He flashes Raquelle a smile and she smiles back, and Smithy thinks: So many wonderful grown-ups out there. They've kept Tris safe for us. And happy. And ignorant. He doesn't know. I don't ever want him to know.

And yet, somebody has to know. If we don't make public what she's done, Cheryl gets away with it.

Their mother used to sing a spiritual. "So high I can't get over it . . . So low I can't go under it . . . So wide I can't get around it . . . Oh, rock-a my soul."

No, God, Smithy dictates. We've got to get over it, under it *and* around it.

*   *   *

On the first pass, Diana does not find the laptop or the briefcase. Methodically, she shifts every box, searching back to the eaves and restacking. When her hair brushes against something, she jerks away, expecting spiders. It's a lightbulb with a beaded metal pull chain. Nice location.

She's trying to come to terms with Jack's theory that his aunt Cheryl murdered Mr. Fountain. Diana can't go for it. She's not comfortable with Mrs. Rand, doesn't approve of her obsession with the house rather than the children, doesn't think planting Tris in front of a TV every waking hour is good for him. Still, Diana is not willing to believe that the woman would commit murder.

As for the docudrama, could Mrs. Rand be making it up? Has Cheryl convinced herself a TV crew wants to immortalize her window treatments?

The laptop and briefcase are tucked so far back under the eaves that professional movers could pack this attic and never spot them. Diana drags them out. If there had been even a teensy-weensy chance that Mr. Fountain's death was not an accident, the police would have demanded to see this stuff. Police always go deep into computer histories. It bolsters her theory that Jack is exaggerating.

Diana restacks boxes to make room for the folding staircase to fold. She pulls the chain of the ceiling bulb and drops the flashlight into the briefcase. Now she's standing in the dark over a coffin-sized opening, the fat leather handle of a heavy briefcase in one hand and a slimline laptop with no handle in the other. The stairs are steep and the little broomstick railing doesn't offer much support. She backs down slowly. It feels tippy. The laptop is sliding from her grip.

There is a sound like gunfire. Diana drops the laptop, which smacks on the oil spot in the middle of the cement floor. What is the survival rate of laptops dropped on cement?

The garage door goes up.

Cheryl Rand is home.

• • •

Tris is showing signs of wear and tear. They need to get out of the restaurant and let him run around and yell. Down the road is the state beach where few people will go on a wet November day. Since Madison doesn't have a car seat, Jack goes once again through the routine of helmet and bike, and sets off for the beach with his little brother hanging on to his belt loops. Madison and Smithy will catch up after Smithy changes her clothes in Dunkin' Donuts' restroom.

Jack pedals in circles around a huge empty parking lot,

waiting for his sisters. It isn't actively raining, but it's misty, and Tris hasn't fully dried out from his last outdoor adventure. When Madison arrives, Jack leans the bike against a pine tree and the boys crowd into her small car. It's very warm. The idling engine hums with a comfy whir.

"Sit on my lap," Jack tells Tris, "while I open your toy car pack."

"No. I want to sit with Madison and Smithy."

The girls are delighted. Everybody switches places. Jack gets in front while Madison and Smithy wedge in back, with Tris squashed between them. Jack doles out the toy cars one by one.

Tris has had a big day and a lot of fresh air. Warm and snug between his sisters, he falls asleep. "If we talk without raising our voices," says Jack in a monotone, "we can cover any subject without waking him up."

There are too many subjects. They don't know where to start.

How did they get here, anyway? The four Fountain children—orphaned, divided, estranged, on the run, using diversionary tactics, hiding out.

"Can we use the television people to our advantage?" asks Jack. "Suppose we show them the photographs and tell them about Madison's discovery in that Jeep?"

Madison snorts. "Talk about a media frenzy. They'll love the idea that the stepaunt framed the toddler for murder. They won't help us find out the truth. They'll just use that along with everything else in their docudrama. This will be serious prime-time stuff."

"Anyway," says Smithy, "Angus asked me how I felt when my mother said she'd rather be dead than bring me up."

"Okay, so we can't trust Angus," says Jack, and they laugh. The laughter helps. They toss ideas around. The girls defer to Jack, because he is the one who stayed. But if they are to be a family again, they have to get back to their old family ways. "You're the oldest, Madison," Jack points out.

"But you're the good one."

He nods. "Second-borns are always superior."

"However, it's the third child who has an intelligent thought," Smithy puts in. "Let's figure out *why* Cheryl would do it. If we want somebody to take a second look at Cheryl, we have to have a reason why she would do it. *I* want to know why she did it. The only thing we've come up with is that she wants the house. But everybody wants a house and a car and money somebody else earned. They don't kill for it. And how would Cheryl know Daddy would get killed? It's more likely he'd jump out of the way, get a scratch and send her packing."

"Suppose Dad was going to send Cheryl packing *before* the accident," says Jack.

"Cheryl did something, Dad found out, and he threatened to fire her?" asks Madison. "That's possible. Maybe Dad found out that she hurts Tris."

"No, because Tris isn't afraid of her."

"Maybe Cheryl was stealing. Spending money on herself that Dad gave her for groceries."

They can readily believe this—especially Jack, now that he

knows Madison gets an allowance and he doesn't—but their father would just have fired her and she would've left.

"We're not going to get anywhere with guessing games," says Jack. "We need a way to scare Cheryl into leaving of her own accord. Suppose we go back to the house and hide out upstairs until the TV crew leaves. Then we confront Cheryl. We show her the photographs. We make it clear that she has to leave."

"I don't think we can scare her, Jack," says Madison. "I think she'll talk her way out of the photographs."

"I haven't seen them yet," says Smithy. "Let me see them."

• • •

Cheryl's headlights illuminate Diana Murray, who is halfway down the stairs with somebody else's property in her hand.

The Lincoln's engine roars at Diana. Is Cheryl going to drive right through her, crushing Diana against the stairs and shoving her into the back wall?

Diana almost scurries back up, but getting trapped in the attic seems just as scary. And the laptop—she can't leave the laptop on the garage floor for Cheryl.

But Cheryl stops her car outside the garage. Heaving herself out of her car, she slams the door behind her. There's strength in the slam, as if she would've caught Diana's fingers in that door if she could have.

Behind Cheryl's headlights, Diana has a sense of other people moving around. Who could they be? "Hi, Mrs. Rand!" she calls. She tries to sound lighthearted and fails.

162

"What do you think you're doing?" screams Cheryl.

Diana makes it down the steps. The pavement feels good. She picks up the laptop and holds it and the briefcase against her chest like laundry. She can't claim this stuff is Jack's. RF is cut into the leather of the briefcase and scratched on the lid of the laptop.

Now Cheryl is inside the garage. She pauses to press the interior control button. The heavy doors begin to close.

Cheryl advances. Her lips are pulled back in a snarl. She does not look like a civilized woman in civilized clothing. She looks like a predator, teeth bared.

Diana is immobilized. The expression on Cheryl's face chills her bones. Has Tris ever seen that expression? Did Reed Fountain see it? Was it the last thing he saw?

In front of a real producer, Cheryl has been unable to produce. No Tris, no Jack. Smithy and Madison vanish. The friendly neighborhood babysitter lies. Cheryl is tricked into driving to a pointless destination. And now the friendly neighborhood babysitter is stealing from her.

The big doors slam down.

Diana Murray is alone in a closed garage with a murderer.

Eleven

DIANA, LIKE EVERY TEENAGER IN AMERICA, POSSESSES A WEAPON.
She uses speed dial. "Hi, Mom. I'm over at Jack's. I'm in the
garage. Cheryl just got here. I'll be home in a minute."

Cheryl stops mid-attack. She can close all the garage doors
she wants, but what happens here will not be a secret.

"Okay." Diana's mother sounds distracted. She's probably in
the middle of a transaction, because she disconnects almost immediately, and Cheryl, inches away, knows.

"You give those to me!" she shouts.

Diana takes giant steps toward the breezeway door, which
opens at a touch, crosses the small space and opens the outside
door with her elbow.

A handsome blond middle-aged guy is blocking the way.
"Hiiiiii," he says, drawing out the word like a party host. "And
you are . . . ?" A big smile fills the bottom half of the man's face.
It's the wrong time and place for a smile that big.

Out on the wet grass, somebody in the settling gloom raises a heavy camera to his shoulder. They are going to record Diana in the act of taking things that are not hers. Will it matter that Jack asked her to? Probably not. A court won't care about a fifteen-year-old's permission.

Cheryl seizes the rim of the briefcase.

What does she think is in this briefcase? Is there some sheet of paper, some file, that Cheryl's been looking for all this time? Is decorating a secondary reason for inching through the house, sifting through every drawer, gloating as she discards the possessions of Reed and Laura Fountain? Diana has always thought there is an element of jealousy in Cheryl's stripping of the house—as if she wants to erase the beautiful situation that once existed there. But maybe she's wrong. Maybe Cheryl is simply protecting herself.

The mist changes to a violent downpour. The blond man, the cameraman and Cheryl flinch.

Diana wrenches free and runs through the pelting rain. Over her shoulder she yells cheerfully, "Bye, Mrs. Rand! Thanks for everything!" Her theory is that on film or tape, her happy voice will deflect the idea that she could possibly be stealing something.

She reaches her car, throws the laptop and briefcase onto the passenger seat, locks the doors and backs out of the driveway.

Then she calls Jack. "Good news, I have the briefcase and the laptop. Bad news. Cheryl caught me."

• • •

The ringtone wakes Tris up. Groggy and cranky from the brevity of his nap, he doesn't want to be with two sisters he doesn't even know. He climbs into the front with Jack and rubs his eyes against his big brother's shoulder. Madison collects the toy cars and hands them to Tris, but he turns his face inward to the comfort of the brother he knows. He listens in to Jack's brief conversation and perks up. "Diana's coming," he says. He scrambles over Jack's lap to reach the door handle. "Diana is my friend," he explains to Madison and Smithy.

* * *

"We're at the state beach," Jack tells Diana, and adds, "Don't let anybody follow you."

"People have been following you? Awesome." Being followed, or following somebody else, is a lifelong dream.

"Not successfully," brags Jack.

Driving toward the beach, Diana checks her mirror. Nobody.

The heavy rain subsides. By the time she reaches the beach, it's drizzling, and by the time she reaches the west parking lot, it's stopped. In the lowering dark of early evening, she just barely makes out Tris running toward her, and Jack racing to catch him. She stops where she is and lets Tris help her out of the car.

"I had donuts!" Tris says excitedly. "At school I finger painted! My painting wasn't dry. We left it there."

Diana often wonders what Tris thinks about. Moments like this amaze her. In the midst of chaos, nightmare, sudden sister appearances and long bike rides in the rain, an almost-three-year-old thinks first of food (donuts) and second of his own

166

accomplishments (finger painting) and third of his own worries (will he ever see his painting again?)

Diana picks Tris up and gives him the circle-swing he loves, holding him under his arms and whirling, so his feet stick out. Then she hands Jack his father's briefcase and laptop. "It wasn't just Cheryl who caught me. There are guys with cameras there. Furthermore, I had to leave the stairs down. Cheryl knows about the storeroom."

"Do you think she'll go up there?"

"Someday, but not now."

Tris leads Diana to Madison's car. Madison and Smithy have gotten out. Smithy looks very young in clothes that are too large and Madison looks belligerent, ready to pick an argument.

Tris examines them briefly, as a visitor to a zoo might pause in front of a habitat. "Those are my sisters," he tells Diana.

The girls give each other tight awkward smiles.

"I'm soaking wet," says Diana. "Do you mind sitting in my car to talk? We can all fit in mine. I need to turn the vent on high and dry myself off a little."

Tris has never sat in Diana's car. He's excited and wants to be the first one in and get the best seat. "It isn't locked," says Diana. "You go on, Tris. Take Madison and Jack."

Diana and her former best friend are alone.

• • •

Smithy knows that she has to start. "I'm sorry, Diana."

Diana doesn't say, "Oh, it's okay." She doesn't say, "It doesn't

167

matter." She says, "It was awful, Smithy. It hurt that you never wrote or called or answered my e-mails. It was mean."

It is a gift of sorts: Diana missed her.

"It was mean," Smithy admits. "But at school I decided never to think. Thinking hurt. You can make a decision not to have thoughts. It's probably like dieting." Smithy has never been on a diet. The Fountain kids are lean. "You just decide to cut something out."

"But you cut *me* out!"

"Yes. And I also cut out my older brother, my little brother and my sister."

"Yell at each other later," calls Jack. "Right now we have to figure out what to do."

◆ ◆ ◆

Madison does not want to be in Diana Murray's car. She isn't clear why Diana is here to start with or why they need her around. This isn't Diana's business.

She forces her mind to the central issue—how to get Cheryl out. They need more leverage than those photographs. They didn't come up with anything that might have happened before the murder, and they can't guess what happened the instant of the murder. Certainly Cheryl will never tell them. Is there a clue in what happened after the murder?

"Come and live with us," said Nonny and Poppy, when Dad's funeral was over. When they had actually lowered a box holding their very own father down into the cold ground.

But if the children had gone to Missouri, they would have left behind every trace of their parents. Somebody would have bought their house. Nobody would be able to tell that Laura and Reed Fountain had ever lived there. Nobody would go into the little woods to see the initials carved in a heart on a tree. Nobody would visit the graves. (Not that anybody does now; Madison cannot stand getting near the graves. The worst thing about burying Dad was reading over and over again the stone next to his: *Laura Courtney Smith Fountain.*)

Again Nonny pleaded. "Live with us."

Aunt Cheryl took the children aside. "Your grandmother is destroyed by your father's death. Your grandfather has health problems. You must not worry them. They're sweet to ask you to live with them, but they can't handle it."

Jack summoned the courage to say, "We'll stay here. We belong here."

But almost immediately, they didn't belong there. Cheryl hired a maid and stopped doing any housework. She stopped cooking and bought dinners at a catering deli. It was her house now, and she was all house, all the time. The kids were treated like furniture, expected to sit quietly against the walls and make no noise.

Somewhat to Madison's surprise, there is a clue in this. If the children had departed to live with their grandparens, Cheryl's free ride would have been over. So Cheryl did capitalize on Dad's death—keeping the kids so that she could keep her job. But that does not mean that Cheryl would kill to keep the job.

Smithy and Diana are trying to catch up with each other. "How long have you had this car?" Smithy asks.

"Dad picked it out for me when school started," says Diana. "I was so surprised. I wasn't sure they'd let me drive at all, never mind give me my own car."

Mr. Murray. Reed Fountain's friend. Close friend. "Diana," says Madison slowly. "Your dad and our dad were tennis partners. They played golf. They barbecued. Do you think your dad might know something about why Cheryl did"—she speaks carefully in front of Tris—"what we think she did?"

* * *

That's ridiculous. How could her father possibly know anything about Cheryl Rand? Diana does not want to bother him. He's still at work. He's like Mr. Fountain—long hours, extra days, big distances. Luckily she can get out of this easily. She nods toward Tris. They are all talking in circles so he won't follow the conversation.

Smithy interferes. "Tris, want to go down on the sand with me and find the best seashell to bring home?"

"No."

Jack tries. "Would you find me a seashell, though? I need one."

"And me," says Madison. "I need a seashell."

Tris looks at Diana, as if she's babysitting and has the last say. This does not go over well with Madison or Smithy. Diana sighs. "Seashells are good," she tells Tris. "I bet Smithy is a good shell hunter."

"I'm a good shell hunter," says Tris immediately.

"Better hurry," says Jack, and once again, Tris vaults out. On

170

her own, Diana wouldn't let him. It's getting dark. The sand will be very cold. The waves will be high and frothy. But Smithy is his sister. It's time for her to be the babysitter and keep him safe.

"Here," says Jack. "Look."

Diana lines up the photographs. She stares them up. Rearranges them. Whispers captions. Then she looks at Jack. "How can you sit here in some stupid parking lot? You should be at the police station!"

"No. We don't want Tris back in the news. We don't want the police, Diana."

They cannot possibly leave the police out of this.

But Jack is a puppy, begging. Diana melts. She adores him, of course, all the girls do. She has the advantage, living so close and babysitting so often. Sadly, in Jack's eyes, she's just a replacement sister. But a girl has to work with what she has. Diana calls her father's cell phone.

"Hey, sugar," his voice booms. "Home from school? How was your day?"

"Hi, Daddy. It was good. Do you have a minute?"

"I have five," he says, and knowing her father, he means this precisely. "What's up?"

"Jack and I were talking and I was sort of wondering. Daddy, did Jack's father ever talk to you about Cheryl Rand? Was she, like, a problem of some kind? To Mr. Fountain in particular?"

"What was your conversation with Jack that you're asking about this?"

"Smithy's back. So everything's on the table again."

"Smithy's back? That's terrific! How's Jack taking it? He's

171

been a trooper and she's been a shit. It won't be easy to be buddies again."

Good thing Smithy is not in the car to hear this. "But I was wondering. Did anything happen the last month or so before Mr. Fountain died? Was he mad at Cheryl or anything?"

"Well, I don't think he was mad, but he was uncomfortable. She began hinting that she wanted to marry him. He was looking around for a replacement nanny or housekeeper, but he hadn't taken action yet."

Marriage? Cheryl thought *she* could replace five-star Laura? It is in Diana's nature to feel sorry for Cheryl, hoping to be a good wife when Mr. Fountain just wanted a good maid.

"Then came the accident," her father continues. "Talk about good luck—Cheryl was still around. Who else was there to take care of the kids? Of course, the grandparents, they wanted the kids, but they wanted them to move to Missouri, and everybody thought it was better for the kids to stay in the same house."

"Everybody thought so, Daddy? Who is everybody?"

"Oh, the psychiatrist and the doctor Cheryl took the kids to."

Diana knows, because she and Smithy were close friends back then, that no psychiatrist and no doctor saw the Fountain kids until much later.

"The doctors felt those poor kids were so traumatized," her father goes on, "that shipping everybody and their stuff across the country would be another death. I have to run, honey. We can talk more tonight."

Diana's phone call is over. She closes her cell phone like a clam shell, as if to hide the news in there.

172

Jack is shaking his head. "Dad? Marry Cheryl? If Cheryl proposed to me, I'd start laughing."

"That could be it," says Madison seriously. "Even I might run over a person who laughs at the idea of marrying me. Maybe they're out there on the driveway, and Dad leans out of the Jeep and tells Cheryl he'd rather be dead than marry her, so she says fine. You're dead."

Jack actually grins. "No. If Cheryl proposed to him in the driveway, Dad would just roll his eyes and drive off. He wouldn't take the time to discuss it."

"I have to agree. Still, it gives us a reason why Cheryl could be mad enough to hurt Dad. Now we need a reason for Dad to get out of the Jeep."

This is not Diana's affair. She should stay on the sidelines. Speak only when asked. But Jack and Madison are so busy figuring out the logistics of their father's death that they are forgetting their immediate situation.

Tris and Smithy appear over the sand dunes, heading back. Diana is embarrassed to find that she is relieved, as if she really thought Smithy would not be sufficiently careful. Then she talks fast. "When Cheryl knows what you have, when you show her those photographs, when she sees there is proof of what she did— you can never let Tris be alone with her again. You can't be alone with her either. Think of every cop show you've ever seen. People who murder once find it easy to murder twice. And you can't discuss this in the morning. In the morning she'll be in control again, and you'll just be kids under her roof. Starting tonight, it has to be your roof. You have to make it clear that she has no choice except to leave. And not only does she have to leave tonight, she has to leave without a scene. Because in the Fountain family history, scenes bring television crews."

• • •

The sun is gone.

The day is done.

They have two cars, a bike and no car seat.

They have a plan, which has little chance of working, but it's all they can come up with. If Cheryl is alone, maybe they can pull it off. But if Angus or the crew is there, they are crippled. "TV is like an occupying army," says Madison. "We'll never get them out."

"A TV crew has to be paid," argues Jack. "Since we never came home to be filmed and since there are probably breaking stories to cover, they're long gone." Jack is lying faceup on the backseat of Diana's car, with Tris lying facedown on top of him. Tris has distributed his gifts of shells and pebbles and is sleepy again. He's not quite out. Jack rubs his back. Please go to sleep.

"Even so, Angus might still be around. And Gwen," says Madison.

"It's four-thirty on Friday. I bet they want their weekend as much as anybody. I bet they're gone."

"I'll call and ask," says Diana. She dials the Fountain house phone. No one answers. Cheryl never lets a phone go unanswered. "It's weird she's not home."

"Probably out shopping," says Smithy.

"When all four of you are missing? When she doesn't know where Tris is and she's selling herself as the loving aunt?"

"Out for dinner, then," says Madison. "Angus took her, I bet."

Jack can't see that happening. The television producer already owns Cheryl; he doesn't need to buy her a thing. And it's early even for early-bird specials. Angus Nicolson seems more like the type to eat dinner at nine o'clock than at four-thirty.

"Maybe they're at the day care, filming," offers Smithy.

"No," says Jack. "We've got the star. They're not going to waste time unless the star is there." Tris's breathing is deeper. He doesn't know he's the star.

"It doesn't matter," says Madison. "In fact, it solves one of our problems. We can get in the house without anybody knowing and we can get started."

Smithy locks Jack's bike to a picnic table. If there is anything normal in their lives in the morning, they will come back for it. Smithy rides with Madison.

Jack folds Tris into a damp little package on his chest. However minor it is—transporting a toddler without a car seat— it would be evidence Cheryl could give a judge; that Jack, Madison and Smithy cannot be trusted with Tris. Maybe they won't be noticed, but the main job of a TV crew is to notice. Diana is driving very slowly, hoping to avoid police attention. In Jack's opinion, she's driving so slowly that she will *attract* police attention.

He doesn't want this confrontation with Cheryl. He's afraid of himself, not her. His anger is swelling and bloating. His hands don't want to pat Tris; they want to strangle Cheryl.

He reminds himself that everything so far is a guess. They don't know anything for sure and they're never going to. Cheryl won't admit anything. There's a faint hope that Dad wrote something down on paper and it's in the briefcase, or electronically and it's on the laptop.

Doubtful. If Dad, for example, e-mailed Mr. Wade about how awkward Cheryl had become, Mr. Wade probably reacted like Mr. Murray and thought how lucky it was that when the accident happened, Cheryl was still around.

Going through that fat, stuffed leather satchel and checking every file in the laptop will be a lengthy task. There is certainly no time tonight. Jack has the passing thought that at least it's Friday. What if he were juggling school tomorrow and homework?

• • •

Madison has no faith in the plan.

And even if the plan works—which it won't—then what? Four kids on their own? Are they going to take on grocery shopping and laundry and banking and changing the oil in the car and measuring Tris's feet for new shoes? Even if they try, the Murrays and the Emmers will figure it out before the weekend is over. No matter what Jack wants, some sort of authority will be brought in. No matter what these authorities decide—whether it's charging Cheryl with murder or scolding the children for being dramatic liars and attention-seekers—the media will be there. Angus will be there. Gwen. The crew.

In fact, whether Cheryl gets away with murder or she doesn't, she'll still get the publicity she wants.

Next to her, Smithy bounces, eager to get started. Madison feels a thousand years old.

• • •

Diana turns onto Chesmore, an unlikely locale for a lurking police car. She whips out her cell phone. "Mom, do me a favor?"

"You do me one. Where are you? You said you'd be home in a minute and you never showed up."

"Did you go over to the Fountains' to look for me?"

"No. Why would I do that? I'm just working away and waiting for you."

Her mother didn't even notice that Diana was stating names, time and place in case of a major crime. So much for protection through cell phones. "I'm sorry, Mom. I've been babysitting for Tris. We'll be home in a while. Mom, would you look out the front window and see if there's any action at the Fountains' house?"

"What kind of action?"

"Oh, you know. Police, fire trucks, TV crews. The usual."

"Diana, you can be so annoying."

"I know. But do it. Please?"

"Fine. I'm walking over to the upstairs window. There are no lights on in the Fountain house. No cars in the driveway. No sirens, no crowds, no picketers."

No lights. This is outstanding news. Cheryl not only turns on every light in every room, she often doesn't turn them off at night.

Diana shivers. Cheryl, who is darkness: is she also afraid of darkness? Because evil knows evil?

"Have you given any thought to explaining what's going on?"

"Oh, Mom, I'm sorry, I wasn't thinking. The best stuff is going on. Smithy and Madison are both home! We're having a reunion. I'll tell you everything later."

"Oh, that's such lovely news! Hug the girls for me. Maybe everybody can come over for lunch tomorrow. Tell Jack I'll make his favorite ham and cheese."

"That sounds great. I'll ask. Bye, Mom." Diana passes the Fountain house. "No car in your driveway," she reports to Jack, whose view is limited to the interior car roof. "Everything is dark. I'm going to park at my house." She bumps over the slight gap between the driveway and the road, and heads up the slope of the driveway, less steep than the Fountains' but longer.

Tris doesn't wake up when Diana turns off the engine. The interior car lights come on automatically, but Jack is ready and has his hand over Tris's eyes. Diana cuts the lights.

Madison pulls up next to them. There is no motion sensor attached to the outdoor lights at the Murray house. As soon as they've doused the headlights, the drive is dark. In the shadows between the cars, Jack uncurls and manages to get out without waking Tris.

This is Olympic-level brothering. This is the gold medal.

Diana wonders if Madison and Smithy have any idea what Jack has sacrificed for his brother.

Their street has something called Neighborhood Watch, which is supposed to cut down on crime. There isn't much around here, but not because the neighbors are watching. If a single neighbor has seen a single thing, they haven't said so. All these treks around the house, in the woods, through other people's yards? Nobody sees a thing. They're at work, they're watching TV, their blinds are pulled, they don't have their contact lenses in. Who knows?

Madison, Smithy and Jack with Tris in his arms wait while Diana walks down the street to the Fountain house. She goes straight up to the front door and rings the bell. Nobody comes. She uses her own key and steps into the front hall. The house is unlit and silent. Cheryl would never sit home alone in the dark without the TV on. She isn't crouching behind a sofa, ready to pounce. Nevertheless, Diana tiptoes into the kitchen. She's intellectually certain that the house is empty, but the kitchen seems full, as if the shadows have weight. She moves through the glass porch and opens the door into the garage.

The folding stair has been folded back up. Cheryl's car is parked beneath it.

Diana leaps backward, shutting the garage door and bolting it.

What am I doing? I looked into Cheryl's eyes. I do believe she could kill. And I'm alone in the dark looking for her?

Diana comes to her senses. It's early for dinner, but just right for happy hour, especially on a Friday. If the TV guy is taking Cheryl out, they went in *his* car. Diana doesn't turn on the lights, which would signal the others to come.

Cheryl could be in her bedroom, which is in back. Its lights wouldn't show from the street.

Upstairs, Diana smells Cheryl's perfume, as if the woman is wafting by. The five closed doors of the bedrooms seem to contain things; awful things, listening things.

The ring of her own cell phone drills her heart.

"What's taking so long?" demands Jack.

"Sorry. There's nobody here."

"We're on our way. Tris is awake," Jack adds glumly.

Diana is at the top of the stairs. Let them go into the bedrooms. She looks down. Jack and his sisters come in the front door. Jack glances up. He is the ghost of his father.

Twelve

TRIS WHIRLS AROUND THE HOUSE, SLAMMING INTO STUFF, falling down and laughing wildly. He had had a ton of sugar, hardly any nap and lots of fresh air, excitement and surprises. He is going to have a meltdown.

When Cheryl gets back, they do not want her to realize that they're inside. They move into the kitchen, where they put on only the stovetop light. They pull the shades and drapes and shut the door from the kitchen to the front hall.

"Tris, you have to hush," says Jack, putting his finger to his lips.

"Hu-u-u-u-shhhh!" screams Tris, loud enough to peel off the wallpaper. He ricochets from one side of the kitchen to the other, loses his balance and falls forehead-first against the rounded wood corner of a chair. He's not cut, but the last remnant of his self-control is gone. Sobbing and screaming, Tris writhes on the floor. "I want lunch!" he shrieks.

Smithy, who wants both lunch and dinner, tries to pick him up. Tris screams and rolls under the table and out of reach.

Madison doesn't even try to deal with Tris. Neither does Jack. He hasn't had anything to eat, either, and if they're going to have something hot and good, he has to fix it. He cannot do one more thing.

Diana squats down, grips Tris's ankle and hauls him out. "You and I are going to fill the tub with water." She lifts him against his will. He kicks. Diana immobilizes his feet as if he's a dog at the vet's and heads for the stairs. "You can have three tub toys. I pick the tugboat, the mommy duck and the measuring cup."

"No! I want the beach pail! And the whole duck family!" Tris sounds like the last person you'd want to live with.

Jack summons a molecule of energy. "This is good," he tells his sisters. "We can't be dealing with Tris. We have to deal with Cheryl. Tris is fine with Diana."

"He should be fine with us," says Smithy.

"You made choices," snaps Jack. "They can't be undone."

• • •

Madison has lost her momentary status as older sister. She is close to hating Diana and even hating Tris, because Diana has no right to be here, and Tris is not lovable right now. Once again Madison has to follow Jack's example. She's sick of how he's always the good guy doing the right thing.

On the counter is an untouched loaf of bakery bread in a paper wrapper. "I'm making toast for everybody," says Madison. "Grab a piece as you go by. Don't worry about getting butter on Cheryl's clothes."

182

One time the whole family—back when they were a whole family; back before Tris—went to London for a week. They didn't stay in a hotel for Americans but in a hotel occupied largely by Brits. Afternoon tea came in a shiny brown china pot, accompanied by stacks of buttered toast and thick jams in little glass tubs. For a long time afterward, the Fountains went on toast binges.

Madison catches her last thought—*back when they were a whole family; back before Tris*—and prays: Dear God, this *is* my whole family. Let me cherish them. Please let me be the good one for a change.

The fury seeps away. Because the bathroom is over the kitchen, she can hear water running in the tub. Thank you, Diana, she says silently. She doesn't mean it, but maybe someday she will.

Even the interior of the refrigerator is Cheryl's. There's no real butter. Mom's cookies were so good because of real butter. Madison gets out the plastic tub of fake butter. She makes perfect toast—golden brown all over—and slathers it on. They are starving and would eat anything anyway.

The three of them lean over the kitchen bar, munching toast, wasting what little time they have. Madison doesn't point this out. She just makes more toast. No matter what they do tonight, they cannot achieve an ending. They can only set up a continuation. If Madison wants this nightmare to end, she has to acquire a grown-up on the team. But who? Who will believe them implicitly, without an argument, without letting Cheryl get a lawyer and a TV station?

Church comes to mind. Mom spent so much time volunteering

and loved her church family so. But the church friends, constantly there when Mom was sick, vanished over time. Once Dad died, they were invisible.

A new thought creases her mind. The edge of this thought is sharp enough to cut her heart. Madison actually whimpers. Jack and Smithy quit buttering toast and wait for an explanation. She shakes her head back and forth, as if to make this new thought splash over the edge and out of her brain. She looks up the minister's phone number.

Smithy and Jack stand close enough to hear.

"Madison!" says Reverend Phillips. They remember his voice. He has two of them: a large forward-motion voice for sermons—even though the church has a fine sound system—and a warm conversation voice, always half laughing, as if the minister has the inside track to a good mood. "I'm so glad to hear from you. The youth group was heartbroken when you left town, but we respected your wish not to contact you. Tell me how you're doing."

"I didn't have a wish like that. Who—um—who told you that?" Her voice is cracking. It was one of the terrible hurts of this year. Why didn't those fifteen kids, with whom she'd spent her Sunday evenings, ever call?

"Why, your aunt, of course. She said the counselors and your other relatives and your godparents decided you would be better off with a fresh start. Mrs. Rand asked me to see to it that—" The minister breaks off. He's not young; he's dealt with human nature for a lot of years. "That isn't true?"

"No." The lump in Madison's throat is so large she cannot say more. Forgetting her plan to acquire an adult, she hangs up.

"It's good that you drive, Madison," says Smithy. "You can run back and forth over Cheryl till she's as flat as roadkill."

Madison vaguely recalls hanging up on somebody else today. This must be what shock does to you; you lose the edges of proper behavior.

Cheryl doesn't lose just the edge of proper behavior, she loses the sides and the center. How incredibly angry she must have been to turn Dad into roadkill. Angry enough to make his little son pay as well. Angry enough to wreak havoc in Madison's life, and no doubt in Smithy's. As for Jack, how has he stuck it out?

She stares at her brother in admiration, but what she sees chills her.

Jack is towering with rage. Literally. He's taller with it, back arched and shoulders expanded. If Cheryl comes in now, Jack will go for her jugular.

This is why you call the police, thinks Madison. So they handle it.

• • •

Smithy and Jack lug the immense flat-TV screen from the living room to the cellar. Nothing will upset Cheryl more than the loss of her TV. Cheryl doesn't do cellars any more than she does the outdoors. There might be mold and crawly things down there. And if it does occur to her to hunt for her television in the basement, they don't think she can get the TV back upstairs. She prides herself on her inability to do heavy lifting.

The local cable provider has twenty-four-hour service. Madison cancels their account. Now there is no backup television in the kitchen or in Cheryl's bedroom. Television is Cheryl's life. They're betting she won't live here without it.

Smithy and Jack head for their parents' room. It was always more Mom's than Dad's, filled with pillows, fluff and comfort. Dad's realm was the outdoors. He loved anything with a ball; anything requiring a bat, a club or an oar; anything where you needed fire (the barbecue) or a motor (the snowmobile).

Cheryl has redone the bigger walk-in closet, once their mother's. Clothing hangs in ranks: shirts and jackets at eye level, pants on a lower rod.

Jack spreads a bedsheet on the floor. Clothing slides quickly off hangers and they haul a mass of it down the stairs like hobos with an especially large hanky. It's remarkable how much can be packed into the car. It takes three trips to empty the closet. Next they attack the big cherry bureau. In another life, the drawers on the left were Dad's and the drawers on the right were Mom's. Jack upends each drawer onto another sheet, Smithy kicks everything into the center, and they haul a fourth load to Cheryl's car.

The bedroom looks as if a rough crowd partied here. Knickknacks, stuffed animals, an overturned side chair and a tiny frilled lamp lie on the carpet.

They take a toast break.

Madison is into Dad's laptop, hunting for more. More what? They don't know. She updates them. "Nothing to report."

Smithy and Jack are getting tired. There's a smaller walk-in closet, another bureau, the desk and the entire bathroom still to go. They almost skip the shoes, stacked in dozens and dozens of original shoeboxes. Then they go for it, emptying each pair onto the sheet and leaving a box mountain behind.

Is this going to be enough? Will Cheryl take her clothes and her jewelry and head on out? Will the loss of television and comfort make her go? They don't care about money. Whatever she has, she can keep. She'll need money to go somewhere anyhow, and the whole idea is to make it easy for her.

They stuff shoes everywhere in the Lincoln. Even to Smithy, the plan suddenly seems ridiculous. What does Cheryl care about stripped closets? She'll just hire somebody to put everything back. This won't frighten her out. She might even laugh. And if she comes in with Angus, what a photo op.

But Smithy flies upstairs with Jack to fill the next sheet. They decide to do the smaller closet, once Dad's. They spread another sheet and yank blouses off hangers.

There, on the floor, previously hidden by a hundred sleeves, is a jewelry box.

Laura Fountain's jewelry box.

• • •

Tris won't let Diana peel off his shirt or take his damp socks off. Diana plunks him into the tub—shirt, socks and all. He forgets his bad mood. Diana swims the duck family toward him. "I see toes!" she quacks. "Tasty toes! I'm going to nibble the baby toe!"

Tris splashes. "You can't see any toes. They're inside socks." He takes the socks off. He doesn't want to miss having his toes nibbled by ducks.

Diana sits on the tub rim, which is almost as uncomfortable as kneeling on the tile, and guides rubber duckies under Tris's knees. He hardly notices when she gets the shirt off and he's bare. The warm water is putting him back to sleep, their only hope if this flimsy plan is going to work. Diana lowers her voice and adds rhythm. "Now the mommy duck takes the baby duck under her wing. The mommy duck takes the second baby duck under her wing. They swim in circles. They swim in rows."

Diana puzzles over the very strong reaction Cheryl had to the mere sight of a briefcase and a laptop.

A possibility begins to take shape in Diana's thoughts.

Diana does believe that Cheryl murdered Mr. Fountain. But she does not believe that Jack and Madison and Smithy can prove it, not to the extent a court requires. But they don't have to prove murder. They just have to prove *something*. Anything. If Cheryl has committed any crime or done anything unethical or immoral, they can get rid of her as their guardian.

Madison can search Mr. Fountain's laptop, and certainly Cheryl was frightened by it. But in Diana's opinion, if there's information to find against Cheryl, it won't be in Mr. Fountain's computer. It'll be in Cheryl's.

Tris's eyes flutter. She supports his back so he doesn't tip over, never a good thing in water. But if she tries to take him out, he'll start screaming again.

She listens to Smithy and Jack, tearing up and down the stairs. Tris is at the comatose end of the energy scale, while Smithy and Jack are at the hysterical end. They can't have finished cleaning out the entire master suite, but suddenly they are shouting on the stairs. "Madison! Guess what we found!" They clomp noisily down, having forgotten that the plan requires silence and dark.

Tris's eyes are closed. He's still upright, but not very.

"I have the biggest towel in the whole wide world," sings Diana. "A big big big big towel. We're going to wrap you up like a mummy. And then you and I are going to be spies."

Tris watches Saturday-morning cartoons. He knows what spies are. "Who do we spy on?" He can't even lift his lids halfway.

"We're going to be computer hackers."

Tris loves computers but only at the library is he allowed to touch one. At home, they are forbidden. Even Jack will yell if Tris dares to touch his computer. Tris drags his eyes open. He doesn't want Jack mad at him.

Diana soothes him. "We're going to spy in Aunt Cheryl's computer."

◆   ◆   ◆

Their mother rarely wore costume jewelry. Her few pieces are real. She liked to wear the same ones every day. They buried her with her thin silver cross on its narrow silver chain.

This is Mom's jewelry box from when she was little. When it

opens, it plays the Nutcracker Suite, while the tiny china balle-rina circles, her slender pink leg gracefully extended. Smithy wants to wind it before she opens it.

In the kitchen, Smithy and Madison hover over this find. Smithy winds slowly and carefully, using the fat key that sticks out the side. Then she sets the box on the kitchen counter. Smithy got to wind it, so Madison gets to open it.

The music of tiny bells begins before the lid is fully open. The ballerina springs up and begins to twirl. Smithy realizes now why she characterized Kate as the ballerina on the jewelry box.

Through her tears, Smithy examines the jewelry. She and Jack have yet to clear out the bathroom, where Cheryl's jewelry spreads over the long counter, lies in the shallow top drawer and hangs from little plastic trees. Smithy may have to check all of it, make sure none of it is Mom's.

· · ·

Jack has no jewelry memory. He can picture his mother's smile and hear his mother's voice, but he cannot picture her wrists or throat or earlobes. Did Mom wear this stuff? Jack can't prove it.

Then he frowns. He pushes Smithy's hand away. He's in his nonbreathing mode.

He dumps out the envelope of prints. Shuffles through them. Chooses two.

In the photograph where Cheryl's fingers clutch the brake, her right hand is ringless.

In the photograph where Cheryl has not yet reached into the Jeep, but is standing outside the window, her right hand touches the glass and she is wearing a ring.

The ring lying in this box.

* * *

Diana winds the bath towel around Tris until his arms are trapped and he is swaddled, like a newborn. How much time before Cheryl, and perhaps Angus, returns? If they went to a restaurant, dinner would last a while. But Cheryl's company is tiring. Diana thinks they went for a drink, and will be back shortly.

She turns off the bathroom and hall lights, and walks in the dark to the master bedroom. Cheryl's bedroom is chaotic. But Smithy and Jack have not yet reached the desk. Cheryl's computer sits untouched.

Diana is holding Tris upright in front of her, a cylinder of thick toweling, easy to hold. Inside the towel, he'll be very warm. Maybe he'll fall asleep instead of demanding a turn at the keyboard.

No such luck. "I want to turn it on," whispers Tris. Whether it's the coffeepot or the sound system, he wants to push the buttons. If Diana says no, he'll raise his voice.

She frees his little right arm, lets him start the computer and then tucks his arm back in. "You're all bare," she whispers. "You have to stay inside your towel or you'll freeze to death. Brrrrrrrr." She walks back to shut the door behind them and turns off the bedroom lights. "Brrrrrrr," she reminds Tris.

She sits, rocking him. "Brrrrrrrr," she sings softly. "Brrrrr." She pulls down Cheryl's list of bookmarks. Cheryl seems to have largely celebrity interests, but one bookmark speaks to Diana.

Cheryl Rand does her banking online.

Cheryl will kill and Cheryl will lie. Diana is betting that Cheryl will also steal.

The bank home page is clearly arranged. Diana clicks Account Access. She enters the user name, which she knows because Cheryl often e-mails to ask her to babysit.

But to access the actual accounts, the bank requires a password. Diana does not have it. She cannot guess it. The bank program is designed to stop a spy.

It works.

• • •

Madison picks up the ring in the jewelry box. Holds it next to the photograph. Hands it to Smithy, who slips it on. "Is it Mommy's engagement ring?" whispers Smithy.

"I think so. Remember how at the end her hands hurt? All her joints hurt, but especially her hands? She wouldn't take off her wedding ring, but she did take off her engagement ring."

"Look inside the band," says Jack. "Are there initials? Dad would engrave it."

"RF," Smithy reads. "LS."

"Because when he gave it to her, she was still Laura Smith," says Madison.

Jack studies the photographs. "So literally, one minute Cheryl is wearing this ring, the next minute she's not."

"I bet Cheryl was digging around in Mom's stuff," says Smithy. "I bet she put the ring on. She really did think Dad would marry her. She had the nerve to wear the engagement ring. I bet when Dad saw it, he was mental."

Madison takes up the narrative. "And they screamed at each other. Cheryl wanted to get married and he just wanted Mom's ring back and she pulled it off and threw it under the car."

"Yes!" shouts Smithy. "And Dad put the Jeep in neutral, yanked up the brake, jumped out and got down under the car to get the diamond back."

They stare at each other. Dad would get out of a car to retrieve the engagement ring he gave his bride Laura. The girls' story line fits. But it's a guess.

It's Jack's turn to hold the ring. His fingers are too big to fit even a little bit into the narrow opening, and he can't feel the engraving.

He imagines his father sitting in that Jeep, about to drive off with his two-year-old. Probably talking to Tris over his shoulder, describing the adventure or errand ahead. Cheryl coming out to the car. Saying something. Dad politely hearing her out. And there on her finger, the ring Dad had to take from his dying wife's hand. His father's fury. "What do you think you're doing with my wife's ring? Give it to me!" Cheryl, ripping the ring off, hurling it away, but all it does is roll under the Jeep. Dad kneels down, trying to see the little glint. Maybe he does see it. Maybe he's way down under the Jeep.

And then the car moves.

No.

Cheryl causes it to move.

Because that's the other photograph. Cheryl, face distorted, thrusting herself inside the vehicle, inches from Tris, seizing that brake.

They pass the ring around again.

Only the stovetop and the computer screen emit light. The buttery smell of the toast fills the air. They're alone with their guesses, the image of their father and this jewel of their mother's.

The distinctive sound of a key in a lock is their warning bell. Cheryl is home.

The front door opens. They hear her voice, the one she does not use with the children. "Thanks again!" she trills.

Jack's hands are hot and taut. His loathing for Cheryl spreads into his heart, like fast-moving poison from a tropical snake.

The front door closes. Cheryl snaps the dead bolt. A moment later, a faint white line appears under the kitchen door. Cheryl has turned on the hall light.

She will not go upstairs. Whether or not she's just eaten dinner, Cheryl will come into the kitchen and prepare a tray of snacks. She'll carry it into the living room and sit in front of the large-screen TV.

She'll get a surprise.

That was the plan, anyway. They meant to be upstairs, silent and hiding, waiting for her shock when she sees the empty wall; waiting for her to run upstairs; cornering her in her stripped room; forcing her to see that they are serious.

The snake in their lives opens the kitchen door and feels around for the light switch.

Thirteen

THE ESSENTIAL JOB OF A TODDLER IS TO WATCH EVERYTHING grown-ups do. "It's on the back of the computer," says Tris sleepily.

Sure enough, Diana's searching fingers find a small square of paper taped behind the screen. On it are written three passwords. One looks assigned—a clutter of numbers and capital letters. Diana enters this one. The bank accepts it. She and Tris are looking at Cheryl Rand's bank accounts.

"Tris, you are the best spy in the whole wide world," whispers Diana, still rocking. She switches lullabyes. She was getting tired of *brrrrr* anyway. "In the whole wide world," she sings softly.

Tris is fading. Fading. And he's out.

What is it about a sleeping child that breaks your heart?

Now that Tris is utterly limp, in that complete way of sleeping children, Diana wants to weep for everyone. For Laura Fountain and Reed Fountain. For sisters who needed help to stay and didn't get it and somehow weren't tough enough to hang on without it. For a brother who soldiered on. For a baby who still knows nothing.

The Tris protection team has doubled in size now that Madison and Smithy are home. But the danger to Tris has doubled too.

In fact, Diana may be in danger. She's definitely on shaky ground. She doesn't have Jack's permission to invade a bank account, let alone Cheryl's permission. And when Cheryl gets home and sees the desecration of her precious room and wardrobe, she'll go crazy.

Diana opens her phone and positions it on the desk. If she needs to call 911, she wants it right there waiting for her.

The cameraman, who filmed her taking a briefcase and a laptop, had a good idea. A person should be able to prove when and where she's doing something. If Diana films herself, her phone will record the day, hour and minute. If this ends up in court (where else can it end?), Diana may want proof that she's part of the Jack/Madison/Smithy team, not just some passing babysitter vandal.

Cheryl has four accounts. Two checking, a savings and a money market account. Diana brings up the last ninety days of checks and debit card transactions in the first account. Household money, because the electric bill and the maid get paid from this account. A big round number is being deposited each month, probably the household allowance from Mr. Wade. Anything that's left—and there's a lot left—is transferred to the other checking account, which receives a monthly deposit of its own. Most debits on this second account are to women's clothing

197

stores. So that one is Cheryl's personal checking, in which her salary is automatically deposited, and into which she shifts money from the household account.

Is Cheryl taking money meant for the children? Diana can't tell, but Mr. Wade could. She glances at the savings account—very nice. And the money market—impressive.

Perhaps Cheryl arrived with this much money. Perhaps she's selling things, such as Tris, in order to get it.

Diana locates Mr. Wade in Cheryl's computer address book. She's met him. Mr. Wade drags himself over now and then, trying not to look at Tris, whose mere presence horrifies him. Mr. Wade gives the house a cursory glance, tells Cheryl how lucky the children are to have her and hurries away. He's visibly grieving for his friend Reed, and wishing he were not involved.

You're involved, Diana thinks. She downloads everything to Mr. Wade.

* * *

Madison slides off the barstool. She may need to use it like a lion tamer, to keep Cheryl at bay. Or Jack.

Smithy guards the back door. They don't want Cheryl going out that way. She has to leave by the garage, taking her car with her.

Jack keeps the kitchen island between himself and Cheryl. He grips the edges as if planning to wrench it off.

Cheryl takes one step into the kitchen. Her long strong fingers with their dead red polish are still on the light switch when she realizes that Madison, Smithy and Jack Fountain are standing there, staring at her. She is motionless. Madison is reminded of nature films. Prey have two choices—freeze or run. She and Jack and Smithy are stalking; Cheryl is freezing.

We've got her, thinks Madison. Jack was right. We can scare her.

But Madison is mistaken.

Theatrically, Cheryl puts her hand over her heart. "What are you doing, hanging around in the dark? You're such funny children. I hope you're going to be nicer to Angus than you were today," she adds; lightly scolding, half smiling. "Jack, there was no soccer game. I called the school. The constant lies make me so unhappy. I've been telling Angus what a burden it is, dealing with you. Angus has promised to interview your guidance counselors and teachers, so we can get to the bottom of your behavior. Well, we can think about that later. Have you had dinner? What would you like to have?"

She's posturing, thinks Madison. Practicing for when Angus is here recording, when the person she wants to impress is listening.

"Look at these photographs, Cheryl," says Jack, more calmly than Madison expected.

Cheryl pays no attention. She turns her back, establishing that she is not even slightly concerned, and opens the refrigerator to study the contents. Then she opens the side-by-side freezer. She removes a pack of frozen hamburger patties and a sack of frozen rolls. They clunk like rocks against the counter.

"In this photograph, which Tris took on Dad's cell phone, just before Dad died," says Jack, "you are standing outside Dad's Jeep. You're wearing a ring."

Cheryl turns slowly. Her eyes do not rest on the photograph. They fasten on Jack. Madison is suddenly deeply afraid. This is not a woman they can scare. This is a woman to be scared of.

Cheryl turns her back again, without bothering to glance at the photograph Jack holds up. She slams the frozen meat against the counter to break the patties apart.

Jack opens the jewelry box. Cheryl whips around to see the source of the sweet tinkling tune. The ballerina circles gracefully. "You've been in my room," whispers Cheryl.

"This is our mother's jewelry box. You took the engagement ring Dad engraved for her. You were wearing it the day you murdered our father."

Cheryl freezes a second time. Then she giggles, sounding eerily like the tinkling music box. "Nonsense. Madison, do the Emmers know you're here or are they worrying about you?"

"They know I'm here."

Jack holds up another photograph. "Tris's fingers. Proof that he's holding the cell phone and taking the pictures."

"You're pretending the cell phone play of a baby might mean something?"

Jack holds up the next photograph. "Your hand, Cheryl. It's around the parking brake. Those are your fingers, your nail polish color. But no ring, Cheryl. You've thrown it away by the time you murder our father."

Cheryl smiles kindly. "Of course you wish that Tris could be innocent. But he isn't. Madison, put these in the microwave and thaw them."

Madison tries to be the one giving orders. "Cheryl, it's time for you to leave. We've packed your things. They're in your car. You need to start driving."

"You touched my things?" The smiling lips shudder and spread in an odd reptilian way.

How lucky that Tris was so demanding, energetic, sometimes cranky and bratty. How lucky that Cheryl handed him off to day care or Jack.

Cheryl has set her handbag on the island. Jack takes her key ring, removes the house key and puts the car keys back. "Time to go, Cheryl. All we want is to get you out of our lives. We're not calling the police, even though these photographs are proof. They're dated, right to the minute. There was never an accident. There was a murder. But all you have to do is get in the car and drive away."

"Nonsense," she says. "It's a shame Angus isn't here to record this. He's never found a more dysfunctional family. It will make quite a portrait when you start talking like that. But go on practicing. Angus will think it's great theater. And as for the keys? I have another set, of course."

They can't make her go. Even if they can herd her into the garage, they can't make her drive away.

In the weight of the silent moment, the refrigerator hums. Freshly made ice cubes drop down. The furnace cycles.

A rhythmic whooshing sound begins. It's upstairs. It's easy to identify. It is a printer, churning out pages. The only printer in this house is on Dad's desk—now Cheryl's. Up in Dad and Mom's room—now Cheryl's.

For a moment all four of them are puzzled. What's printing? They don't have a fax, so there is no situation where something can print by itself.

"Who is up there?" says Cheryl, in a low fierce voice. "Who is touching my computer?" She bolts from the kitchen and with unexpected speed races up the stairs.

They have allowed to happen the one thing they agreed must never happen: Cheryl will be near Tris.

Smithy flies after Cheryl, Jack on her heels.

At the top of the stairs, Cheryl is howling.

Madison has the horrifying sense that they have arrived, finally, at the place where they will fight it out.

She must not let Jack hurt Cheryl, nor Cheryl hurt Tris. She must do whatever it takes to stop one brother and save the other, even if it destroys her. She has a glimpse of what her mother went through: you do what it takes, even if you go down doing it. She is awestruck by her mother's guts.

Cheryl is flying into Mom and Dad's room. Smithy, Jack and Madison fly after her. The bedroom lights are not on. Only the computer screen gives off a sickly glow.

Diana sits in front of it. The printer on her left is spewing copies. Tris is in her lap.

Cheryl Rand launches herself at Diana.

• • •

Diana hears them coming. Who couldn't hear four sets of feet pounding on the stairs? Cheryl is screaming, "Who is that?" Jack is screaming, "Get back here!" Smithy is just screaming.

Impossible to hide, so Diana doesn't try.

In spite of her momentary terror in the garage, Diana is not expecting an actual attack from Cheryl. But the big woman throws herself across the room as if to crush her. Diana swivels the chair, offering the strong molded back to Cheryl, and sticks out one hand to make a quick cell phone adjustment, hunching over Tris to keep him safe.

The force of Cheryl's body flings the wheeled swivel chair forward. Cheryl smashes to the floor, while Diana is ejected from the seat. Diana plays volleyball, field hockey, softball and tennis. She's strong. She simply steps up and out of the chair as it spins forward, so gracefully that Tris does not stir from his sleep. She circles the floundering Cheryl, who has hit her face against the desk edge and is bleeding. Diana gets her cell phone and moves behind Jack.

One thing Diana can be sure of: there is stuff in this computer that matters, whether or not it's the stuff she forwarded to Mr. Wade.

Cheryl hauls herself to her feet. A queer jumbled expression is on her face, a messy laugh coming out of her mouth. "I'm calling the police. You hurt me. I can prove you are dangerous. I'll get rid of all of you at one time."

She fumbles for the house phone by her bed. She does not seem to notice that the bed no longer has sheets or blankets.

"Not yet, Cheryl," says Diana. "I filmed you." She forwards the tiny movie to her mother's phone for safekeeping and then passes the phone around, so that everybody has a turn. Cheryl's turn is last. In the short video, Cheryl Rand bears down on a sleeping child, sharp red fingernails extended, lips pulled back from her teeth. She looks like some ancient hideous Medusa, taking revenge or going insane. She looks like a killer who uses her bare hands.

Downstairs, musical and soft in the front hall, the doorbell rings.

• • •

Cheryl's face smooths out. Her posture returns to normal. She smiles. "It's Angus. He had a little errand to run and he's coming back with papers for me to sign."

She walks through them and heads for the stairs as if nothing else exists. Only the possibility of television exists.

Fourteen

CHERYL IS ACTUALLY SINGING A SORT OF TRA-LA OF TRIUMPH AS she dances down the stairs.

Madison races to get between Jack and Cheryl. There's no time for a conference and Jack is tipping over the edge. Down the stairs is where they want Cheryl. Close to her car. Away from Tris.

But what to do about Angus?

Madison doesn't want Angus in the house. But she doesn't want a shoving match with Cheryl either, and Cheryl will reach the door first.

• • •

Diana retreats to Tris's bedroom. She plans to lower him slowly and carefully into his crib, but once she's in the room and has shut the door behind her, she can't bring herself to set Tris down. What if they have to run? What if Cheryl and Angus come up here?

Tris's damp hair curls against his cheek. His little mouth is open, and his even breathing is soft and sweet.

How innocent he is. He did nothing; he knows nothing.

But things have gone sour.

Cheryl's wound makes it worse. Cheryl will win. Television will capture this little boy forever in a cold, convincing film.

She can't even call her parents. Cheryl has her phone.

Diana feels amputated.

•   •   •

Cheryl throws the front door open.

Nonny and Poppy walk in.

They take no more notice of Cheryl Rand than of the nearest maple tree. Smithy hurtles toward them, elbowing past Madison and Jack. When Nonny holds out her arms, Smithy dives into her embrace. "Oh, Nonny, you came! I wasn't even nice. I didn't even talk to you when you visited my school last summer. Here you are anyway."

Cheryl comes to an uncertain stop in the doorway. She wavers, staring at the dark yard, sure that Angus must be out there somewhere.

"Of course we're here, darling. Your school phoned this morning. Your headmistress was concerned, Smithy. And her phone call with Cheryl was disturbing. There's something radically wrong, Dr. Dresser told us. Get on a plane. So we did."

Jack comes to a halt on the very step where he stood this morning, listening to the plans of Angus and Cheryl. Everything violent dissipates. That is his grandfather smiling up at him. That is his grandmother holding Smithy.

Nonny wipes away Smithy's tears. "Is it that bad?"

"Not now that you're here. How did you get here so fast?"

"Darling, this isn't the eighteenth century. We got a three-hour direct flight. We were just boarding when we got a second call. It was from your roommate, Kate. Get on a plane, she said, there's something wrong. Smithy's afraid for Tris."

Jack reaches the last step. He is taller than his grandfather. But oh, the wonder of it—his grandfather is a grown-up. *He* will be in charge. *He* will handle Cheryl.

"I didn't even answer Poppy's e-mails or your postcards, Nonny," says Smithy.

Their grandfather's voice is so much like Dad's that Jack's heart clutches. "All the more reason to come. Everything was wrong, and there we were in another state, wringing our hands because our feelings were hurt. How stupid is that? If everything is wrong, the grandparents should at least wring their hands in the same house as the grandchildren."

It has never occurred to Jack that the feelings of grandparents could be hurt. He could have made an effort. But he was all efforted out.

Madison makes it into her grandparents' circling arms. "Cheryl told us you were too old and ill to help."

"Nonsense. We're middle-aged and slow to understand. It's late in the day. But we got here."

"I think you made very good time," protests Smithy.

"On the plane, yes. But over the whole year, no. When we

207

came last summer, and you children were scattered, we should have rounded you up like lambs in the pasture and brought you home. But we didn't. Somehow we couldn't get to know you." Their grandfather smiles. "We will this time." He and Jack have reached each other. His grandfather grips Jack's forearm and shoulder. For a moment Jack feels as young as Tris.

He pulls himself together. "There are problems," he tells his grandfather. "The first is television. Cheryl sold Tris to TV. She's got a producer to do a docudrama portraying Tris as a monster. It's scheduled. We don't know how to stop it. The second thing is that after all this time I looked in Dad's cell phone. You know how he always took pictures. What we didn't know is that Tris took pictures too. Tris took the very last pictures. It's proof that—" Jack cannot quite say out loud to Dad's father how Dad actually died.

"We haven't seen those pictures," says his grandfather, "but we've been on the phone with Mr. Wade since we picked up our rental car at the airport, so we've heard all about them. You sent them to him, remember. It took him a while to figure out the significance. It wasn't until he studied the date and the hour that he understood. He's at the police department as we speak."

Jack's heart stops. The police? Everything he dreaded is going to happen? More attention on Tris? More publicity?

"Trust us," says Poppy gently. "We'll handle it. Tris will be all right."

Jack is seized by a curious joy. It isn't happiness. Jack is not happy. It's deeper and more extraordinary. All this time, through all this suffering, all he had to do was call his grandparents.

I'm the kid again, thinks Jack. The grown-ups decide. I don't have to shoulder it anymore. People Dad and Mom loved will decide. Even if it goes in a direction I don't want, I get to be fifteen.

Jack feels weirdly lightweight, as if he's entered a different wrestling category.

And he has.

Kids play sports. He can be on a team. Of course, he's grown so much. His arms stick out farther than the last time he competed in anything, his legs are longer, he's out of practice, he'll be useless—but these are just things to work on.

"Your dad would be so proud of you, Jack," says his grandfather.

"I don't know if he would. I don't know if I handled things very well."

"You never let go of your brother's hand. Now, where's Tris? Nonny and I want to reassure ourselves that all is well."

They jump at a sudden rumbling metallic sound.

"It's the garage door," says Smithy. "Cheryl is leaving, just the way we planned."

Poppy shakes his head. "She's not going anywhere. I parked the rental car up against the garage door."

• • •

Tris's grandmother bends tenderly over the sleeping child in Diana's arms and tucks the towel back from his chin.

Diana tries to explain. "There wasn't time to get him into pajamas."

"This is perfect," says Nonny. "And so are you, dear. Let's put him down in the crib. We don't have to keep guard."

"Cheryl might—"

"Cheryl won't be doing anything. The children's grandfather will see to that. And you were so wise to download that paperwork to Mr. Wade. He could tell in a minute that Cheryl is fiddling with the accounts. He'll show that paperwork to the local police along with the cell-phone photographs."

"Jack doesn't want the police," says Diana anxiously.

"What Jack wants is to protect Tris. And now we're here, and we'll protect him. Something we singularly failed to do before. Let's go downstairs."

• • •

Through the open front door walks Reverend Phillips. He's a big man with a big voice, and he more than fills the space Cheryl left. He looks around. "Hey, Maddy," he says cheerfully.

"Maddy" sounds good coming from him. Maybe she can be Maddy again, be the nice reliable laughing person that girl Maddy was once.

"I got worried when you hung up on me," says Reverend Phillips. "What's going on?"

Madison tells him everything. The minister is more shocked than anybody. "I believed her. I believed everything she said."

"We all did. You wouldn't believe some of the stuff we believed. But the police are on their way. Mr. Wade is talking to them."

And then, incredibly, Cheryl is back, offering cheese and

crackers on a tray. She can't leave, so she's going to tough it out. "How nice of you to drop in," she tells the minister.

"Mrs. Rand, under the circumstances, I do not want you around the children," says Reverend Phillips. "You and I—"

Cheryl falls back on tears. She points to her bruised mouth. "Those children ganged up on me. They're liars. I tried so hard to bring goodness into their lives and look at the thanks I get. They twist an accident into something ugly."

"What was accidental," asks the minister, "about blaming Tris?"

And then Mrs. Murray is bounding up the front steps, and in the front door, holding out the tiny terrifying film of Cheryl attacking Diana. She's much thinner and smaller than Cheryl but the force of her wrath flattens Cheryl against a wall. "What is this?" she demands at the top of her lungs.

Cheryl is cornered: Mrs. Murray, Reverend Phillips and Poppy. Jack takes advantage. "Call Angus Nicolson," he orders Cheryl. "Cancel your arrangement."

"Oh, I can't do that. They're planning to film on Monday."

Poppy uses a voice Jack has never heard before. "Call," he says to Cheryl. "Now."

Cheryl dwindles. She seems to lose weight and color and purpose all at the same time. She takes out a cell phone, and stares at it, puzzled, forgetting that it is Diana's. She knows Angus's number by heart and slowly taps it in. She tries to keep her options open, but Angus is a professional. He cuts his losses. "Okay," he says. "That's that." He disconnects and all Cheryl Rand has to show for her efforts is a dial tone.

"I'll just go upstairs," begins Cheryl.

211

Tris is upstairs. Jack steps forward, his fears and fury back again.

The minister gets hold of Cheryl first. "Mrs. Rand, you and I are going to wait outside for the police."

"This is my house! I'm not giving it up. You can't make me."

"It is not your house. We'll wait outside."

"It's raining!"

"Then we'll get wet." Reverend Phillips shoulders Cheryl into the cold.

•   •   •

How strange it will be, thinks Madison Fountain, to finish senior year in yet another school.

It's not what anybody wants. But Madison has figured out the order of things. First you want your family safe. Second you want your family.

She opens her cell phone and pulls up her favorite photograph of her mother. She hasn't looked at it in a long, long time. But there her mother is, waiting for her.

Jack did his best, Madison tells her mother. I let you down. But I'm on the right track now. And Tris is fine. Isn't that amazing? Tris is fine.

You'd love Tris, Mom.

You'd be glad he's alive.

•   •   •

Smithy realizes that the house no longer matters. It isn't Mom and Dad's anymore. It's okay to leave.

Home won't come to us, she thinks. We have to go home. Nonny and Poppy's.

She's grateful for a semester and a half of boarding school. She has learned that there are good friends everywhere, waiting for you to appear. Distant as Missouri sounds, it will be the same: full of kids waiting to be friends. And Smithy will have her sister and her brothers, and the grandparents who love her no matter what.

Cheryl was treasure hunting, looking in a film, in fame, in a bank account. But treasure is where your heart is, and that is your family, and Elizabeth Smith Fountain is a lucky girl.

She has a family.

*   *   *

Tris sleeps on.

He doesn't know about the troubles surrounding him.

He doesn't care where he lives. He just wants a kiss in the morning, and a big breakfast, and time to play outdoors.

But one day he will know that he is blessed by two big sisters and one big brother. He is loved.

CAROLINE B. COONEY is the author of many books for young people, including *Diamonds in the Shadow; A Friend at Midnight; Hit the Road; Code Orange; The Girl Who Invented Romance; Family Reunion; Goddess of Yesterday* (an ALA-ALSC Notable Children's Book); *The Ransom of Mercy Carter; Tune In Anytime; Burning Up; The Face on the Milk Carton* (an IRA-CBC Children's Choice Book) and its companions, *Whatever Happened to Janie?* and *The Voice on the Radio* (each of them an ALA-YALSA Best Book for Young Adults), as well as *What Janie Found; What Child Is This?* (an ALA-YALSA Best Book for Young Adults); *Driver's Ed* (an ALA-YALSA Best Book for Young Adults and a *Booklist* Editors' Choice); *Among Friends; Twenty Pageants Later;* and the Time Travel Quartet: *Both Sides of Time, Out of Time, Prisoner of Time,* and *For All Time,* which are also available as *The Time Travelers* Volumes I and II.

Caroline B. Cooney lives in Madison, Connecticut, and New York City.